OUT FOR THE HOLIDAYS

AN OUT NOVELLA

CARA DEE

D1113129

Edited by Silently Correcting Your Grammar, LLC.
Formatting by Eliza Rae Services.

CAMASSIA COVE

Camassia Cove is a town in northern Washington created to be the home of some exciting love stories. Novels taking place here stand alone unless otherwise stated, and they will vary in genre and pairing. What they all have in common is the town in which they live. Some are friends and family. Others are complete strangers. Some have vastly different backgrounds. Some grew up together. It's a small world, and many characters will cross over and pay a visit or two in several books. But, again, each novel stands on its own, and spoilers will be avoided as much as possible.

Out For the Holidays *is the sequel to* ***Out****, a novel taking place (partly!) in Camassia Cove. If you're interested in keeping up with the characters, the town, the timeline, and future novels, check out Camassia Cove's own page at www.caradeewrites.com.*

AM I DOING THIS DEDICATION THING RIGHT?

PROBABLY NOT, NO

Really, there's a purpose to this message.

Equality is on my mind. We don't have enough of it.

So let's fight harder next year, okay?

I hope you'll have an amazing holiday, by the way.

Sincerely,

The awkward writer of this comedy

CHAPTER 1

LET IT FUCKING SNOW

Zach Coleman

Finally home.

I idled in the driveway by the river and looked up at the house, exhausted and wondering if I could get Henry to carry me in. I could see him up there, the sight drawing a tired smile from me. Our house—or maybe big-ass lodge was more appropriate—had all the woodsy coziness we could want. It sat on a steep mountainside and was built on top of our garage. If the weather report was anything to go by, it was gonna be the perfect setting for a holiday card.

We were surrounded by forest-covered mountains on three sides and the river on one. The large windows of the living room faced the half-frozen water, and I watched as Henry stacked boxes of Christmas decorations on the floor by the windows.

He'd picked out a tree already—without me, dammit—and it was waiting to be decorated in the corner.

"Indeed, Clark, and with the harsh winds coming down from the Canadian interior, we can count on..."

I killed the engine, effectively silencing the radio too.

1

Yeah, just let it snow.

This Christmas had to be better than our first one. Hell, next *year* had to be better than our first one. We could look back on it now and shake our heads in amusement, but goddamn, *nothing* had gone according to plan.

I should've known we would have to rethink everything when Brooklyn hired me the first time. There was no such thing as spending the "summer and fall" in Camassia and winter and spring in LA.

We were supposed to have spent the holidays in our then-new home last year. Instead, we'd gotten stuck at LAX because of me and a goddamn photo shoot. Snowstorms, a strike, and general delays had pushed our departure from early Christmas Eve to the first flight out on Christmas Day. We'd eaten our first Christmas breakfast together in United's lounge, just Henry and me, while Mattie and Ty had driven back and forth to pick up Nan and then us when we landed in Seattle.

This year was gonna be different. Henry and I had promised each other to lay off work all of December; it was gonna be our vacation before Mattie and Ty came home on the twentieth. Martin was flying up the day after too. It was set in stone. Nothing was gonna keep us from celebrating the holidays at home, hopefully with a lot of snow falling, with our loved ones.

With a heavy sigh, I started the engine again and rolled the car into the garage. I had to talk to Henry about my schedule, and I hoped he approved. Mattie and Ty already knew because they'd been there when I'd had a minor meltdown the other day.

We'd spent Thanksgiving in LA since Ty and Mattie went to college there and I was working, so though it'd only been a week since I saw Henry, I missed him. It seemed to have become the running theme. We were always missing one another because even when we were together, we were so tired.

I was kinda done with that.

I parked next to Henry's Jeep. He'd become lumberjackier up

here, and when I'd asked what he was gonna do with his Lexus, he'd said it had no business in Camassia. Here, he wanted a Jeep for off-road driving.

Mattie's and Ty's cars were parked on the other side of the center path. Waste of money, if you asked me. They didn't live here anymore. One car would've sufficed for them, but no, fucking Martin had given each of them new wheels for Christmas last year.

I climbed the stairs and dug out my keys, though I doubted the door was locked. This wasn't LA, and we had two dogs now too. We were safe and protected by one sharp Chihuahua and one goofy Rottweiler. It was supposed to have been the other way around...

The smell of home hit me with enough force to make my eyes water as I stepped inside the hallway. Henry had Christmas music playing, and the man was baking something.

"Baby? I'm home." I dropped my bag on the floor, smiling as the dogs came to greet me. "Hi, my pups." I squatted down and picked up Lady. Not like Lady in that Disney movie, but like *First* Lady. Little Lady Mo, if we were going to get technical. "Did you miss me? Oh yes, you did."

For being two completely different breeds and sizes, they were sort of similar. Lady's coloring was the same as Diesel's.

Eagle didn't greet anyone like this. Unless Henry and I were making him exercise, he supervised everything from the couch in the living room. Sometimes, we were allowed to cuddle him, Henry more so than me. Possibly because he gave Eagle tuna on the sly.

Henry finally appeared, and the dogs were momentarily forgotten.

I threw myself into his arms and breathed him in.

I felt him smiling against my neck.

"I was wondering how long you were going to sit out there in the car," he murmured, hugging me tighter. "Christ—it's so good to have you home, darling."

"I'm hoping we get snowed in." I eased back enough to get his lips.

"Mmm, apparently there's a risk of that. I hope so too." He deepened the kiss. "I saved you some food from lunch, and there're fresh rolls for you."

Fuck, I loved him. Last Christmas, we'd decided to buy something together. It led to the adoptions of Diesel and Lady through Brooklyn's husband's rescue dog organization. Then, 'cause Henry was a sneak, I'd spotted something with my name on it under the tree. So I'd run out and bought the bread maker he'd been eyeing.

It was the gift that kept on giving, and every time I came home from LA, there were these amazing rolls stuffed with cheese and garlic waiting for me.

"Will you nap with me?" I asked.

"But it's December now, sweetheart. I have to decorate the house." He was too fucking adorable sometimes. "I didn't get to do this last year."

I remembered. He'd been so upset, and it'd been hard not to laugh.

"It'll be different from now on," I promised. "I'll go shower and nap after I eat, and then I'll help you decorate. Yeah?"

He hesitated. "Are you qualified?"

I stared up at him blankly. Then I shrugged out of my leather jacket and snorted, leaving his decorating diva ass behind. I'd probably never grasp how he could be so full of authority, dominance, and masculine hotness ninety percent of the time and then flip to a fussing mother and housewife with extremely high standards the other ten.

It was only one of the reasons I was so in love with him. Whether he was making plans to go hunting with friends he'd made in town the past year, or he was quoting Oprah, the man kept me on my toes.

The cobwebs of sleep clung to me as the dreams shifted and changed, the images blurring. I frowned. My cock was engulfed in wet heat, the strong suction drawing a drowsy groan from me. *How is this... I mean... What's...* I grunted, rousing from sleep slowly. My dick thickened and grew harder. Oh God, it was Henry. I wasn't having a dinner meeting with Brooklyn.

A sleep fuck, oh yeah. I wasn't gonna move an inch. This was exactly what I wanted after the hectic weeks I'd just had. Actually, I was gonna move, but only to give him more access. With a sleepy sound, I ended his fantastic blow job and served him my ass on a platter. I rolled onto my stomach and drew up my leg, then sighed contentedly and let the exhaustion grab on to me again.

Henry breathed a curse and carefully spread my cheeks, his strokes gentle and dirty. The fantasy of him taking advantage of me while I slept got me off at record speed every goddamn time.

"I missed this pretty little asshole," he whispered. A finger brushed over my opening, and I suppressed a shiver. His pinkie finger wriggled inside, just the tip. Then he replaced it with his tongue.

I exhaled heavily and buried my face in the pillow.

He tongue-fucked me sensually, his movements always measured.

I gave the mattress a sleepy thrust to get some friction for my cock.

This had become my absolute favorite way to get fucked after we'd been apart. It slowed down my thoughts, centered me in a way, and it was heady as hell. Withholding groans and pleas meant that my energy was contained inside me until I came all over the sheets.

Henry lubed his cock and rubbed himself across my hole, stretching me for his pleasure. The head pressed deeper, then disappeared. My dirty bastard loved to watch.

I stayed still. The feeling of being possessed this way was indescribable.

When he was buried all the way in, the traces of sleep were long gone. Goose bumps spread across my body, and I stifled a moan.

"My perfect baby boy," he whispered as his lips ghosted over my shoulder. His hard cock filled me unhurriedly, over and over, and I shifted again. My leg came down a bit so his thrusts would inch me up and down along the mattress. "It's been a while since you woke up in a wet spot." He scratched my scalp gently, carefully pressing my face into the pillow. "Filthy boys like you just can't help but come in your sleep."

Oh, fuck.

His thrusts came faster, and my cock was rubbing against the sheet persistently.

He dipped down and bit my shoulder, soothing the sting with a swipe of his tongue. "Christ… Who knew I'd fall in love with an exquisite ass whore who takes my cock so greedily."

My whimper was muffled by the pillow. The pressure built up, my breaths turned shallow, and it was getting difficult to stay relaxed for him. My muscles trembled with the need to tense up.

Henry fucked me harder. The friction of the sheet and my own stomach sent me closer to orgasm, and he increased the pleasure by slipping a hand underneath me to fondle my balls.

"Oh, they're full and ready, baby," he murmured, out of breath. "Time for you to make that mess. Just like I'll make a mess inside you."

Without being allowed to make a sound, I swallowed my groan and felt the pressure boiling over. He rolled my balls firmly and fucked me into the mattress, and that did it. *Ungh.* I grunted and gnashed my teeth together, the climax taking over. My cock released in spurts just as Henry started coming.

I slid through my own mess, my dick and stomach coated in come.

"Oh God." Henry shuddered violently and rested on top of me, his labored breaths hitting my shoulder in hot puffs. "I needed that."

"Me too," I rasped, and it wasn't over. I'd grown to need the cuddles that followed almost as much as the sex. In a way, it was a moment that put me back together. "Can you stay inside me?"

"Of course, my darling." He shifted us so my back was to his chest and we were on our sides. Then he held me tightly as the last few months' tension drained out of me. "You've been stressed out for quite a while now, Zachary. Are you sure it's not too much? I worry when you work so hard."

No, I wasn't sure anymore. It had kind of snowballed this year. Brooklyn's holiday campaign last year had aimed a spotlight on me, and I hadn't been prepared for shit. It was still surreal and bizarre to see myself on actual billboards, and there *were* fucking billboards, holy hell.

In the span of four months, I'd gotten a real agent, though Martin loved to play famous person and travel with me. I'd seen New York, Miami, Chicago, and Austin. I'd been catapulted into this crazy lifestyle, and the shine was wearing off fast. This summer had been the worst. Even as we were all together in our house in Santa Monica, I'd lost my footing. The boys had spent their days on the beach or taking care of Henry's bookstore, Henry had taken on a big project at Second Family, and I had... for lack of a better word, floundered.

"I've made a decision," I murmured, getting sleepy again. Now that I was in Henry's arms, I could relax. "It was a mistake to work with others." And that was what I'd started doing in June. My agent had called me; a fashion designer wanted to book me, and I'd shrugged and said *fun*. Which was bullshit. "Brooklyn's kinda made a family of her models, and that's fine with me. She's not crazy, unlike that photographer I worked with in Long Beach."

"I remember you were upset." Henry kissed my hair. He'd had to come visit me on set almost every day, because I wasn't cut out for it. The hours were mad, the demands were fucked up, and it just unsettled me. The money wasn't worth it. "But you enjoy being a spokesmodel for ShadowLight?"

Yes and no. In August, my social media had exploded because Brooklyn's team created a YouTube channel for the three models who were the main faces—Akira, Maliah, and me. We were featured in videos and behind-the-scenes footage from shoots, and that sort of attention was different. There were suddenly people who commented and followed me.

"I like the shoots," I admitted. "I don't mind that my face is everywhere either, but the social media shit makes me uncomfortable. Did you know it's in my contract that I can't make my Instagram private?"

I'd gone from sixteen followers to sixty-seven *thousand*. And it was growing every day. It freaked me out. I didn't want any part of it, not like that.

Henry propped himself up on his elbow so we could see each other, and he furrowed his brow. "You said Martin had a lawyer look it over. Didn't they explain everything?"

Yeah, well. What the fuck did I know? It'd sounded good at the time. "I didn't think it was gonna get so crazy, Henry." Did I just whine? Christ.

"Oh, my sweet man," he chuckled and stroked my cheek. "Tell me what I can do for you. I didn't know things were this bad."

It wasn't really. "It slapped me in the face when you left after Thanksgiving." I'd been thrown into a quick but hectic shoot with a friend of Brooklyn's, and then I'd come home to Mattie and Ty. Henry wasn't there, and I'd lost it over seeing an email with new accounts created for me on Facebook and Twitter. "I… It's not who I am. I like posting a few photos here and there on Insta and seeing what my friends and family are up to, but that's it."

Henry nodded slowly, pensive. "We'll get your contract renegotiated for you after the holidays, then. You should talk to Brooklyn. You don't want to blindside her with this." That made sense. She'd done a lot for me. "What else can I do?"

I sighed contentedly and pressed my back to his chest. "I guess I want more structure. A routine. The going back and forth so much isn't fun. The other week, I forgot what fucking month it was."

He smiled sympathetically. "That's fair. I miss having a routine too. I like being settled."

"*Yes*." That was the word. I wanted to be more settled.

I wasn't the only one who had a lot to do either. Henry had more balls in the air than a gay porn star. Since we got together a year and a half ago, he'd become more involved in Second Family. He'd become a donor at a nonprofit organization that helped men, women, and children escape abuse right here in Camassia too. And this was on top of his side gigs with whatever investments he was making, the world's most unsuccessful bookstore in Malibu, and coming to my aid when my photographers were cunts.

"I'm more at home here," I admitted. "We automatically plan to spend holidays here. It's here we hang our pictures on the wall…" Not that we didn't have photos in Santa Monica, but more often than not, it was a place to crash. Mattie and Ty obviously loved it there; it was their full-time home while they were in school. For me, though…? "We put more care into this place too."

"I agree." He lowered his head and kissed me softly. It was… yeah, a contrast to the fact that he also shifted his softened cock deeper into my ass.

I smirked.

He wouldn't be deterred; he stayed on the subject. "I have to admit, I've come to see this as my primary home. It's...private and just ours."

That was how I'd felt too. Henry had found the lodge only a couple weeks after coming up here, though there'd been renovations. New kitchen, slamming up walls here on the second floor, fixing the guest bath downstairs. Now we had four rooms upstairs—three bedrooms and Henry's office. The open living room and kitchen took up most of the downstairs, and I had been frustrated with Henry for taking so long to *get it right*. It was just a place to cook and a place to watch TV or make a fire, right? Or not.

Now I was glad he'd been meticulous and a raving perfectionist because it'd turned into a home I could see myself sharing with Henry for the rest of our lives.

My fingers traveled along his arm that was locked over my stomach, and my thoughts wandered to the lonely attic. I had given up the pretense of taking shit slowly a few months after Henry and Ty had moved in. Mattie had told me he and Ty wanted to turn the attic into their man cave. Mattie's brain and heart had already lived here, even then. It was a matter of moving his stuff, and then he was set. So I'd terminated our lease on the apartment shortly after, and that was that. Henry welcomed me home to where I belonged, and then we almost got caught fucking in front of the fireplace. Good times.

"Maybe we should let Mattie and Ty take the attic now?" I glanced back at Henry.

"Hmm?" He tilted his head.

I shrugged a little. "Just sayin'... They're only here for some breaks, and we could turn their rooms into something else. Rich people always have home gyms. Or...you know." I cleared my throat. "A kid's room?"

The look in his eyes softened, and his mouth twisted up at the corners. "You want to talk about adopting?"

I was getting there, that's for certain. "Soon...? Yeah. What about you?"

"Well," he sighed, then smiled ruefully. "I'm not getting any younger, my dear."

I snickered and kissed his chin. "You're forty-seven, not eighty." Given how old his entire family was, he'd probably outlive me at this point. His decrepit grandparents hadn't passed until way into their nineties, which didn't bode well for us where Henry's parents were concerned. For all I cared, they could drop tomorrow.

"That will be fun," he mused. "I'll join the ranks of Hugh Hefner and date my young model."

My shoulders shook with laughter, something he obviously felt, because he groaned under his breath and pressed his crotch harder against my ass.

"I don't think Brooklyn wants me around in thirty years," I said. "Shit, I don't want that. Maybe another year or two, tops."

Henry hummed and kissed me with an underlying current of hunger. "You'll always be my model. Let an old man keep his fantasy."

"You're so fucking dirty. I love you."

I couldn't say that enough. We were allowed to have our superficial fantasies too. Lord knew I did. I got off on our differences: his experience, his laugh lines, his scruff that glinted silver here and there...it was all so fucking sexy to me. And it made me stick my ass in the air for him to claim, kiss, fuck, and smack.

It also turned him into the hottest bottom. He didn't find himself in that mind-set often, which suited me perfectly, but when he did? Sweet Jesus, I couldn't go more than a day without bending him over and ramming my cock inside him. He begged shamelessly and commanded his little boy to fill his asshole—I groaned at the images flooding my brain. In a way, he was in charge even then, 'cause I did as he said. Like some insatiable slut.

"Where's your head, boy?" Henry demanded huskily.

I bit my lip. "Given that I can literally feel you getting harder, I think our minds are kinda synced."

"Perhaps so." He smirked faintly, wickedly, and gave me a sweet kiss. "Have I mentioned how happy I am to have you home?"

Once or twice, though he could say it over and over again.

CHAPTER 2

I DON'T WANNA

"Zach! This is a surprise." Nan smiled and muted the TV in her room. "What brings you by?"

"Henry kicked me out." I smirked and dipped down to kiss her cheek. "Apparently, I'm not qualified to help him decorate the house."

He'd put up with it yesterday, and we'd had a fucking perfect evening of drinking spiked hot chocolates, listening to Christmas music, decorating the tree together, and making love in front of the fire. Today was a new day, and he'd kindly suggested I go see Nan while he finished the rest.

He was gonna redo the tree.

Nan nodded as if that made complete sense. "He does tend to struggle with you a bit there."

Oh, whatever.

I sat down next to her bed, studying her, and shrugged out of my jacket. She looked better after having been down with a vicious cold most of the fall. It had fucked with our Thanksgiving plans, 'cause we'd wanted her to be able to see LA. She'd been bummed about not being cleared to go, but we'd take her next spring instead.

She wanted to see the Ferris wheel on Santa Monica Pier and have ice cream at sunset on the beach.

"I see they helped you decorate already." I saw there were Christmassy drapes, a red quilt on her bed with a bunch of miniature angels, a small tree on the table by the window, and little Santa Claus knickknacks all over. "Who brought you flowers?" There were two arrangements in the window. A lot of red, a little white, plenty of green; I remembered Amaryllis and Poinsettia from Henry's cute ramblings, and even I knew holly.

"My future grandson-in-law, of course." Nan smiled affectionately at the flowers. "Henry did this yesterday. He came over with a delicious beverage that tasted like Christmas. We chatted."

I could only guess he'd brought chai tea. I'd learned he only had that for Christmas. "Wait, he decorated too?"

"Mmhmm." She was nodding and nodding. "He's such a lovely man, sugar. Why haven't you proposed yet?"

Not this again. I knew she adored Henry; hell, she'd been a fan from the first time they met. And it was mutual. Maybe he loved her more than me, 'cause *fuck* if I knew why we weren't engaged.

"I told you. He doesn't want me to," I muttered bitterly. "Since I brought up the kid thing, he wants to be the one who proposes." It was part of the truth anyway. He'd asked me to forgive him for his "chauvinism" and that he felt it was his "honor."

I had no issues with that, as long as he popped the damn question before *I* got grays.

"Oh. Well, perhaps he'll propose on Christmas." She patted my hand. "Tell me how the boys are doing. Mattie told me he's tired."

I nodded. My brother had been studying hard to keep up perfect grades for as long as it'd been required to hold on to scholarships. "Ty's doing great. He loves his classes, and he spends most weekends at the bookstore. But yeah, we're gonna talk to Mattie when they come home in a few weeks. I think he feels pressured to do better, so I don't know. Maybe he should drop a couple classes."

He hadn't turned nineteen yet. He had time.

Henry was studying menus in the kitchen when I came back home. We were both cooking more when we were in Camassia, but Henry had a preference for appetizers. If he got his way, every main course was ordered in while he made snacks and appetizers from scratch.

"Hey, gorgeous." I'd heard an upbeat song on the radio right before pulling into the garage, and it made me restless. I walked up behind Henry and kissed the back of his neck. "I miss dancing with you."

He sent me half a smile over his shoulder. "You're the one with the amazing moves."

No way. "Come on," I coaxed. "We have three weeks to ourselves. We'll go stir-crazy if we don't get out of the house at least once."

He chuckled. "Of course we'll go out. I was thinking we could do a weekend in Seattle."

"Yeah?" I grinned and bobbed my head to an imaginary beat, my hips moving. "You'll take me dancing?"

"If you take me to a show."

"Deal." What a crazy bargain. We enjoyed both, though his love for going to plays and shows was way more developed than mine. I was a newbie.

Doing things with Henry, dates and stuff, was part of what I lived for. Especially since I'd started making more money. We would never be completely equal, but I felt better being able to pull my weight. I took care of the mortgage on the house in Santa Monica, and I could take my man to any dinner he wanted. One day, I'd be ready to do the merging of money shit that Henry enjoyed sighing dramatically about.

My phone rang, so I stepped back and pulled it out of my pocket.

"Indian okay for dinner?" he asked, going back to the menus. "I thought I'd try my hand at making naan bread."

"Sounds great, baby." My thumb hovered over the accept button. It was Brooklyn calling. "I'll do Nan's meatloaf for us tomorrow—okay, fuck. I won't avoid you, Brooklyn. Christ, it's like she knows." I put the phone to my ear and punished Henry's chuckle at my expense by squeezing his junk. "What's up, hon?"

Henry grunted quietly and covered my hand with his.

"Pull up your pants and tell Henry to tuck away his monster," Brooklyn ordered. It was nothing near what we were actually doing, but I released Henry's cock and felt like I'd been caught all the same.

She sounded frustrated, so I left the kitchen and walked through the living room. There was privacy upstairs in Henry's study.

"Something's up," I said, taking two steps at a time.

"Yeah, you can say that. Why aren't you in Cancún?"

Could I fire someone via text? I was so pissed that I didn't know what to do with myself. I'd returned to the first floor and planted my ass at the bottom of the stairs, and I was staring at my agent's number in my phone.

Lady Mo was in my lap, comforting me.

To my relief, Brooklyn wasn't angry with me. She knew I took bookings seriously and never showed up late. No, this was on my agent, who hadn't fucking told me she'd booked me for a whole goddamn week.

I released a breath and rested my head in my palm. Lady nuzzled my cheek.

If it'd been any person other than Brooklyn, I would've canceled somehow.

"Can I ask what you're doing, Zachary?"

Dammit. I looked up, cursing the windows. Even when he was in the kitchen, he could see me in the reflection. "Can't you tell I'm hiding?"

"Poorly," he noted. Rounding the long bar in the kitchen, he passed the living room and joined me by the stairs. His hands went into the pockets of his slacks. "You have bad news."

"I'd use the words fucking awful, but whatever." I forced myself to look up. He'd be so disappointed. "Amanda neglected to tell me about a week-long shoot."

He sighed, then nodded once firmly. "With Brooklyn, I assume."

Yeah. She was the only one I had a contract with now, so it'd been a matter of scheduling.

"Tell me what to do," I pleaded. "I swear I didn't know. I even told her I wanted December free."

He waved a hand and sat down next to me. "You're not on trial, sweetheart."

"I know, but it's always my job that fucks shit up for us." Lady left me, so I leaned forward, resting my elbows on my knees, and rubbed a hand over my mouth and jaw.

"You're in an industry where things change quickly," he reminded patiently. "What I do is very different." True. He sat down with his coworkers and associates twice a year to hammer out details and schedule events and whatnot. It meant he knew his travels at least six months in advance so he could coordinate his schedule between the jobs he was involved in. "Tell me about the shoot."

Reluctance filled me. I felt spoiled for complaining, but after this year... *All* I fucking wanted was a quiet month at home with Henry. "It's for the YouTube crap. Akira, Maliah, and me—we have a week in Mexico, and they're gonna 'capture our personalities' or something. Basically, a small film crew is gonna make a bunch of videos with us in various locations. It doesn't have much to do with ShadowLight and makeup, so I don't see the point." Of course, their products would be mentioned, but focus was on us.

"Marketing, darling." He scooted closer and rubbed my back soothingly. "The clips make you relatable to the consumers. YouTube probably has a far greater outreach than billboards. Up there, you're untouchable."

I side-eyed him. "Didn't know you studied marketing."

Humor flashed in his hazel eyes. "I may have spent some time in Los Angeles in my day. You pick up on these things."

I huffed under my breath and faced forward again, and my gaze landed on the Christmas tree. It was beautiful, and *someone* had already put some gifts underneath it.

"We were supposed to stay home, though. Or at least in Washington." I rested my head on his shoulder. "I wanted to go Christmas shopping in Seattle, go see a movie, take you and Nan for dinner... We were gonna go to a club and dance all night."

He hummed and pressed a kiss to my hair. "You know where I can take you dancing?"

I shook my head.

"In Mexico." There was a smile in his voice, and I admit his confirming that he was coming along brightened my mood more than I could say.

"Thank you for coming with me," I whispered.

He laughed softly. "My beautiful man. I'm not entirely selfless. I trust you with all I am, and I may have gotten over most of my insecurities, but I am not letting you be alone with Joseph anymore."

I grimaced. He was right. I didn't wanna confront Joseph on my own either, and he was the head of makeup for this sort of thing. Brooklyn rarely traveled. She sent Joseph and his obnoxious flirting.

"Are you gonna talk to him?" I wondered.

"Yes. I've cut him too much slack. I should've talked to him months ago."

I put my hand on his leg, sensing the tension in him. It was harder on him, I bet. He'd known Joseph for a decade; they'd started Second Family together and been close friends.

"What's Martin saying?" I asked, 'cause there was no way he didn't know. I didn't mention anything of this to Martin, but Henry told his best friend everything.

"That Joseph needs to back off, of course," he replied. "I'll talk to him."

I nodded slowly, hoping it wouldn't bring us drama. The silence was comfortable, and as I gathered my thoughts and started making mental notes on what I needed to do, snow began to fall outside. Just great.

"We'll be back before Christmas." Henry pressed a kiss to the side of my head, knowing me too well. "You'll get your snowball fights."

I smiled.

"When are we leaving?" he asked.

My smile was gone. "Brooklyn postponed the shoot forty-eight hours, so we gotta be on a plane tomorrow."

He nodded and gave my leg a squeeze. "Leave this to me, baby. I'll find us an evening flight so we can have lunch with your grandmother."

"You're the best." I kissed his cheek.

CHAPTER 3

WELL, THIS IS ALMOST LIKE HOME,
EXCEPT NOT AT ALL

"*M*exico? That's it. When I grow up, I'm becoming a model," Mattie groused.

I chuckled tiredly and sat down next to Henry. "I don't recommend it, but you have fun with that." Checking the nearest clock, I saw it was three minutes until we boarded. We'd made it to Houston where we had our connection, and Henry was using the time to argue with another co-founder of Second Family.

"Okay, you've checked in now. I gotta go, Zach."

"You have class?" That made me check my watch again.

"Oh. No. But I gotta go see someone about a drum set."

I held the phone away from my ear, brow furrowing, and made sure it was my brother I was talking to. Mattie had never shown any interest in music before. He was all about math and technology.

"Did I hear that right?" I asked.

Apparently, he was serious, and he didn't have time to talk about it now.

All right. Pocketing my phone, I leaned back and tapped my fingers along my thigh. Henry was still arguing with Marisol at Second Family. She was in charge of daily operations, and they were hiring someone to work for her when she went on maternity leave.

"I wouldn't go there either," Henry said, pinching the bridge of his nose. "No—because his idea of manual labor is delegating. He's a funder like me. You need someone who knows real work." He paused, listening, and I wasn't sure comparing himself to whoever was a good idea. Henry got his hands dirty on a daily basis when he worked. "What about Joseph? I know he's a silent partner, but he knows protocol. He should be able to help you for a few months."

Hey, I wouldn't mind that. It would take him away from my job.

"Well, I'd talk to him if these interviews don't work out," Henry said. "We're boarding now, but I'll check in when we get to the resort." He smiled, then chuckled. "Of course. You take care of those cravings now. Let me know if there's anything you want me to send you."

I stood up and grabbed his bag. I'd checked a bag with all my shit, so I didn't have a carry-on. Henry was more of a businessman and wouldn't go anywhere without his laptop.

Next stop, Mexico.

Stepping out onto the balcony, I breathed in the sea air and listened to the waves rolling in fourteen stories below. The night was pitch black, except for the bright turquoise of the illuminated swimming pool on the hotel's terrace. It was huge and had an island bar in the middle.

It was nice to finally be here, but it wasn't the smells of pine and snow I'd longed for all fall. It wasn't Christmas here. It was a tropical paradise.

"Are you standing out here brooding, Zachary?" Henry came

up behind me and held me to him, his chin landing on my shoulder.

"No?" I grimaced. "Maybe. I'm sorry."

"I think perhaps you're not seeing the possibilities." He turned his head and kissed my neck. "Come with me." Threading our fingers together, he led us into the living room of our suite and picked up the remote to the flat screen. "You wanted me to take you dancing."

"In Seattle," I said.

He ignored me and found a music station on the TV that played a sultry salsa remix, and the room filled with the sex of music. "So I'll find us a cantina away from the tourists." He hauled me close swiftly, a firm hand on my lower back. I sucked in a breath and looked up at him. "I'll seduce you," he murmured in my ear, "with the best food and sangria, with a hand on your thigh, and filthy whispers that still make you blush." Oh Jesus Christ. He brushed the backs of his fingers down my cheek, and I swallowed hard. "There it is."

I slipped my hands up his biceps, but he only allowed one hand there. He grabbed the other and clasped our fingers.

"When you're wearing that tipsy grin," he went on in a low voice, "I'll show you what foreplay is on the dance floor. We'll be outside, under the stars and string lights, and you'll follow me."

"You'll lead me."

"I'll lead you." He teased me with a kiss at the corner of my mouth as the heavy, almost lazy beat of the song ramped up the tension. The seductive notes of the guitar made me shiver. My cock responded rapidly, and there was no way he couldn't feel it. "Move your hips with me, darling boy." He trapped his thigh between my legs and pulled me closer.

"Fuck." I couldn't not grind against his thigh, if only a little.

Henry slid a hand up my throat. "We won't finish until you're begging me to come."

"Okay." I shuddered. "I guess, um, Mexico won't be so bad."

His smirk was full of promise. "It won't be, no."

"Time to get up, Zach."

"Five more minutes," I grumbled into the pillow.

"You said that ten minutes ago." He crawled over my legs, shifted down the sheets, and bit my ass.

I yelped. "Prick!"

He smacked the spot. "Is my boy turning into a diva? Get your lazy ass out of bed, Zachary. You're going to want breakfast before work."

I lifted my head and looked over my shoulder with a weak glare. "I'm not a fucking diva."

"Then stop acting like one." He folded up the sleeves of his white linen shirt that he wore with tan cargo shorts. I wasn't gonna wear much other than trunks and a beater, so I hoped he could put my stuff in his side pockets. "Come on, up you go."

I groaned and rolled out of bed, my feet hitting the carpet with a thump. "Why are you such a morning person?"

"Why are you such a brat?" he asked, amused. "You're far more disciplined when I'm not around. Martin gives me reports, you know."

"You mean he gossips." I rolled my eyes and stood up, stretching my arms above my head. At least I got him to eye my morning wood. "Wanna come here and suck me a little?" I gripped the base and gave myself a stroke.

He stared for another few seconds. "I... Well..." He shot me a strict, narrow-eyed look. "Get dressed."

I grinned.

Then I took a quick shower, jerked off to the thought of him fucking me, and got dressed.

Fifteen minutes later, we were in the elevator down to the buffet area on the terrace, and he called me a slut.

"Fuck you, it's your fault." I pushed down my shades from the top of my head. "You didn't give me cock last night."

He hummed. "I was more tempted to give you ass, to be honest."

"Why didn't you?" I complained. God, if he was getting into one of those moods, I wasn't sure I'd get much work done while we were here. "I love topping you."

"I know," he sighed. "You were just so sweet and obedient, and the desire to bottom catches me off guard sometimes. I don't want to throw you."

Screw that bullshit. Stepping closer, I grasped his chin. "You're overthinking this, Henry. You're also forgetting that I get off on being thrown. It turns me on when the switch surprises me." I leaned forward and kissed him, the doors opening behind me.

"You're right," he whispered.

I nodded and linked my fingers with his.

Walking through the expansive lobby of the hotel, we spotted a few from Joseph's makeup crew, and I saw Akira talking to her girlfriend near the revolving doors leading to the street. I gave her a wave, then nodded toward the beach. She gestured she'd be right there.

"Noah and Julian are here," Henry said, surprised.

Hell, I was surprised too. I followed his gaze, spotting the couple having breakfast with Maliah on the terrace. They'd scored a table close to the pool, so we made our way between all the other tables to reach them.

"Fancy seeing you handsome devils here." I grinned when Julian looked up, and he smiled widely. "Why didn't you tell me you were coming?"

"Last-minute thing, and we thought we'd surprise you." He stood up, and hugs were exchanged between the four of us. Maliah was on the phone, so that would have to wait. Julian flashed me a teasing grin. "Of course, we didn't expect you to be two days late."

"Yeah, guess who's firing his agent," I chuckled. "We'll be right back, just gonna get food."

"Try the shrimp omelet. It's goddamn amazing," Noah said with his mouth full.

"You're the worst vegetarian ever," I told him.

He waved me off. "Never claimed otherwise, kid."

Henry and I went inside again to where the buffet was set up, and we filled our plates, plus one bowl of fresh fruit we could share, and he got a cappuccino while I got juice.

On the way back to the table, Henry spoke up for only me to hear. "What are the chances of them being here to babysit Maliah as a favor to her father?"

Oh, I'd say it was almost a certainty now that I thought about it. Brooklyn was chill about her daughter being a model. Maliah was responsible and had graduated high school with honors, not to mention sweet as hell. But Asher could never unclench.

"I wouldn't bet against it, that's for sure." I assumed Brooklyn and Asher had their hands full with work and their younger daughter at home. Asher did otherwise take time off to travel with Maliah.

Henry and I sat down next to each other at the round table just as Maliah resurfaced from a phone call that made her sigh heavily.

She was on my other side, so I reached over and kissed her cheek.

"How's Daddy?" I asked her.

"Don't get me started." Apparently, she took my greeting as an invitation to use my shoulder as a pillow. "In his eyes, I'll always be the gangly preteen I was when he met me. Mom keeps telling him to calm down, which, for some reason, is his cue to be overbearing behind her back."

I chuckled and tucked into my omelet, and Noah had been right. This shit was golden.

"I can't wait till you meet the man you're gonna marry," I said around my food. "I wanna be there when you introduce him to Asher."

"Ay, oh, whoa." Noah reverted back to his East Coast origin, although I was pretty sure there wasn't an Italian fiber in him. "She's way too young for that. Christ, Zach."

"So you *are* here to babysit Maliah," I laughed.

"How did you figure?" Julian's mouth quirked in amusement. "I'm on her side, for the record. Uncle Noah can do all the babysitting. I'm here for the free vacation."

I pointed to my man. "He guessed it. Makes total sense."

"I don't want to quote Brooklyn or anything," Henry started saying.

"But the macho men in my family need Jesus?" Maliah drawled.

Noah and I barked out a laugh, and Julian groaned and facepalmed.

She had a point. It'd taken me months to establish a friendship with Maliah 'cause Asher was always there, and I was fucking gay and not a threat whatsoever. Didn't matter to him.

"I was going to say chill out, but that works," Henry chuckled. "If anyone can handle Noah and your father, it's you, dear."

"I'm learning from the best," Maliah replied with a smirk.

"Your mom and Sophie?" I guessed.

"Hell yes."

Maliah, Akira, and I were taken to three separate locations around the city after breakfast, and I was relieved Joseph opted to work with Maliah. It was possible he'd heard I was here with

Henry and had a feeling we were gonna tell him enough was enough.

Henry included, I found myself with a team of six people, and we headed out in a van to some underwater caves. The shore here was rocky and full of basins, caves, and...well, death traps. Henry found a shaded spot to read the paper and chat with Martin, and I was ushered to a sliver of the beach that had sand.

I studied the interview questions while Meredith made my face look blemish-free and flawless. One of the running campaign's background models—Tyrese—was gonna be in charge of asking me the questions.

Since I was a shit actor and had told Brooklyn I didn't wanna lie and make up some fake persona, the questions had been adapted for my sake. They involved less makeup, considering I didn't actually wear any in my everyday life, and were more about acceptance and breaking free from stereotypes.

"You look dismayed," Meredith noted. "Close your eyes, please."

I closed my eyes. "It would be too high-maintenance for me to change the questions again, right?"

"Probably," she chuckled.

Rob, one of Brooklyn's assistants, came over and asked if there was a problem.

Tyrese was close behind.

"Last time I did an interview, it was awkward as fuck," I said with a shrug. "None of this comes very naturally for me."

"Yeah, me either." Tyrese lifted a shoulder and folded his arms. He and I were the only two who hadn't gone through the same audition process as the others. Even Maliah had started from scratch.

Tyrese had modeling experience but mainly for sports catalogues. Neither of us knew how to act.

"Wanna defy Brooklyn with me?" I raised a brow at Tyrese.

"Oh God," Rob muttered. "This is going to get me fired, isn't it? You know, Joseph was very specific—"

"Fuck what Joseph says," I said.

"I'm in," Tyrese replied with a slow grin.

It was settled. After some re-planning and discussing what to say, Tyrese and I headed down the rocks, dressed in regular black board shorts, him showing a hell of a lot more bulk than me. We had our cameraman in tow, a few-worded man named Paulie.

I took a swig from my water bottle, and we found a couple rocks that weren't sharper than heartbreak to sit on. We had the turquoise water behind us.

"Don't sit too close to me, man," I said. "I already look like a friendly ghost."

Tyrese let out a rich laugh and chose to share my rock just to be a dick. *Dick*. At least I was a little taller than him. I had to have something working to my advantage.

He unfolded the piece of paper with the questions, and I dug out my instructions—and the reason I hated interviews. I wasn't sure, but "Remember to smile naturally" wasn't natural for me.

"Ready when you are," Paulie said. He pushed play on his phone too, my "signature" playlist playing in the background. It would be edited before posting, but I always had an MKTO song playing in my videos. Brooklyn's choice for me.

Henry trailed down the rocks with a moping Rob.

"We're not doing any retakes," I said. "Brooklyn wants to highlight me and let the customers get to know me? Then they'll get me, blunders and bullshit included."

I was nervous, yet I liked my idea. It was real. And hopefully funny.

"All right, then," Paulie said, holding up the camera. "Rolling. And by rolling, I mean I pushed record."

I grinned and tilted my head to Tyrese.

"That's my cue," Tyrese said and fanned out the questionnaire. "Hey, guys. I'm Tyrese, and it's another get-to-know-Zach day at

ShadowLight. Our boss handed us this form with questions from fans."

"I'm pretty sure they've been properly vetted and approved by the marketing team," I commented. "For instance..." I drew a finger down the list of questions, pausing at the most obvious one. "I don't think any of the viewers are asking me what the best part is about the new ShadowLight primer." Because I'd learned the sales pitch by heart, and I wasn't going there. "Hold on, I'm forgetting something." I pretended to check my own list, and I nodded to myself. "Remember to smile naturally... Right." I sent a megawatt smile to the camera. "There. Moving on."

Tyrese didn't miss a beat. "In the last video, ShadowLight got some criticism because you're a spokesmodel for a makeup brand, but you mentioned you only wear makeup sometimes. Any comments?"

I rubbed my neck, phrasing myself carefully. As much as I wanted to be myself, I was selling something here. And when I couldn't sell a product, I had to be able to sell the brand and the concept.

"I can't speak for Brooklyn Wright, but I don't think she hired me for the makeup," I started by saying. "In this day and age, it's about normalizing diversity and being proud of who you are. I think that's what she's doing—and has been doing since she expanded ShadowLight. So, no, I don't wear makeup in my everyday life, but I'm all over accepting the idea of it and pointing out it's okay if you do." I paused, thinking back on my first time in a gay bar. "When I came to LA, my boyfriend and a buddy of his took me to my first gay bar, and... Let's just say I had one drink too many, and I ended up crashing a bachelorette party. An hour later, I was taking a bathroom selfie with one of the ladies—right after she brushed a streak of glitter on my cheek. It was...a wild moment for me. In a way, I broke up with myself and who I used to be. I started exploring what else I could do that wasn't the norm."

I caught Henry standing a few feet behind Paulie, and he smiled softly at me.

Tyrese stared at me. "I think we do a better job with these interviews when we don't listen to the boss."

I laughed.

"So do you own any of the ShadowLight products?" he asked next.

I nodded. "Oh yeah. The primer I mentioned earlier is actually awesome. I go between LA and Washington so much, and it's two completely different climates. Like most people, changes in temperature, food, lifestyle in general will appear on my face." I shrugged. "It's a great product." I held up my note. "With an alluring smile, I'm now supposed to tell you what's in the primer, but I'm gonna say you can read about it in the description below the video."

"You're a great salesperson," Tyrese told me.

"I appreciate that, man." I smirked. "I'm ignoring the fact that I can see my boyfriend shaking his head at me. Next question?"

CHAPTER 4

LET'S DANCE, JOSEPH

We went on until we'd gone through all questions and had three hours of footage. For a few questions, we sat on that rock. For the next set, we moved to a shaded location so we didn't get burned to a crisp. The last questions, Tyrese fired off while we were having a late lunch on the beach.

For the rest of the week, we were gonna shoot more commercial-style footage where I'd have a lot less freedom. Luckily, I wouldn't have lines there.

"You seemed to have more fun in front of the camera today," Henry mentioned as we got into the van.

Tyrese and Meredith had gone their own way, wanting to sight-see.

"It's the whole script thing that trips me up, I think." I buckled in and leaned back. "How mad do you think Brooklyn will be?"

"Hmm. There will undoubtedly be more editing to do, but I wouldn't be upset if I were her." He clasped our hands on his leg. "You were funny and cracked jokes. That sort of thing will be appreciated by the viewers."

I hoped so.

"What're we doing tonight?" I yawned.

"I checked your schedule, which someone must've updated," he replied. "There's a big dinner with everyone now that you're here."

I should've known. It was almost a ritual of Brooklyn's, to make sure there was a dinner the first night of a new shoot. The longer shoots, anyway.

I assumed it meant Joseph would be there.

The restaurant was off the beaten path about an hour away from the resort and looked suspiciously like the cantina Henry had said he was gonna take me to. We were led through the stand-alone villa where guests dined on seafood and listened to live music, and the patio in the back had been reserved for us. The lights were there, several strings of them attached to the building and poles on the other side of the patio.

Henry explained many places looked like this.

Either way, it was romantic as hell, and I reached up to kiss his cheek.

A long table had been set for all nineteen of us, and as we sat down, wait staff came out with trays upon trays of seafood platters, quesadillas, guacamole, salad bowls, and more drinks than we could possibly consume. Pitchers of sangria glowed red, and bottles of domestic beer sparkled in gold.

Noah and Julian sat down across from us, and Akira and her girlfriend found seats next to me.

Darkness had fallen, and the air held more humidity than normal, according to the weather reports. There was a thunderstorm rolling in sometime later, though Henry said it would probably miss Cancún.

"Aren't we a dressy bunch tonight." Noah twisted the cap off his beer and looked around us. "No wonder you didn't want me to wear my Beavis and Butthead tee, baby."

Julian snorted and shook his head.

I grinned and nudged Henry's foot with mine. "I've been told I don't always have to wear my graphic tees, either." So I'd dressed for my man, and most guys here wore similar clothes. Slacks and button-downs in fabrics for warm weather.

"You look amazing," Henry murmured in my ear.

I stole a kiss.

"You got some color today," I told Julian. He looked slightly uncomfortable too. His nose had a little red shine to it.

"My shoulders are so sore," he confessed.

Ouch.

"You're using it as an excuse not to dance with me later." Noah sent him a narrow-eyed look.

"Not a fan?" I guessed.

Julian sighed, and I got the feeling it was an argument they'd had more than once. "I'm not good at it. He makes everything look so easy, and I just fumble and make a fool of myself."

"And I've told you I don't care about that." Noah leaned in and pressed a lingering kiss to his neck. "Can't blame me for wanting to hold you close, can you?"

I smiled at them, stoked to have them as friends. Learning their history had been a bit of a shock, but they complemented each other perfectly. Julian did struggle with some insecurities, though. Then again, didn't we all?

Conversation lulled while we filled our plates, and I zeroed in on Joseph when Henry quietly pointed out that he kept looking our way. He was seated farther down, closer to the end of the table, with Rob and a few others.

"I'll speak to him tomorrow," Henry said.

It wouldn't surprise me if Joseph told us we were overreacting.

"So where are you guys spending the holidays?" I asked.

"All over, it feels like." Noah filled up on some more chips and guacamole. "Dinner with Julian's grandparents on the twenty-first in Pittsburgh, dinner with Brooklyn and Asher on the twenty-third in LA, then up to Sophie and Tennyson's place in Mendocino for Christmas."

"What about you?" Julian asked, gaze flicking between Henry and me.

"We'll be home." Henry smiled and refilled our wine. "The boys are flying up on the twentieth."

"You'll have to come up and visit sometime," I said.

"Well, yeah," Noah agreed. "Julian and I collect nieces and nephews, and we hear you guys are next. It's my way of teaching children around the country about the glory that is the Penguins."

I laughed, the wine getting to me.

Julian smiled and shook his head, then faced me. "Have you decided what route to take?"

"Adoption," I answered.

Henry gave my leg an affectionate squeeze.

"Two friends of ours adopted," Noah said. "I'll get you their information. I'm sure Danny will wanna help."

"We appreciate that." Henry nodded.

I smiled and took a swig of my wine, realizing we'd become a *we*.

Around us, people were getting tipsier and merrier, and a few couples had taken advantage of the music to get their moves on. Thunder rumbled in the distance, and I shivered when a breeze rolled into the humidity.

"Excuse me for a moment." Henry wiped his mouth with a napkin before leaning close to me. "I've had it with Joseph's stares. I'll be right back."

Wait, so they were gonna talk alone? Without me?

Henry was already gone, leaving me to wrestle irrational jealousy. It wasn't fair to Henry, whom I trusted with all my heart.

Joseph, however? I wouldn't put it past him to try something. He'd certainly tried with me.

Noah had his eyes on the dancing pairs. "What do you say, sweetheart...?"

Julian pursed his lips and shook his head. "Have you forgotten our wedding? I literally bruised your toe."

"Weak shoes." Noah winked.

I drained my glass. Henry was taking Joseph aside, and I clenched my jaw when they disappeared from sight around the villa. Needing a distraction, I turned to Noah.

"I'll dance with you," I said. "I'll give it one song before Julian's all over you."

Julian gaped at me. "You're supposed to be my *friend*, Zach."

I puckered my lips at him.

Noah smirked and stood up. "He's being a friend, Julian. I also think he's right. Let's go, kid."

He rounded the long table and met up with me at my side, and I followed him out onto the floor as an upbeat song started playing. We didn't have live music out here. Instead, we had a mix CD, and I recognized this one. A Santana collaboration with the dude from Matchbox Twenty.

I placed my hand in Noah's extended one, and he took me by surprise when he spun me around before hauling me close. "Holy shit," I blurted out in a choked laugh. "Okay, I guess you know what you're doing."

Noah grinned. "My sister taught me when I was little."

"Good to know." Yeah, Julian didn't stand a chance once he interrupted, and I knew he would. "Lead away, Prince Charming."

And fuck me if he didn't. The rock song brought more people to the floor, and soon most of us were getting a workout. Noah made it fun with unexpected dips and twirls, and it'd been a while since I laughed so hard.

"We should just form a circle around you," Akira hollered over the music. "Goddamn, Noah."

Sweat beaded on my forehead, and I got into it. I had to hand it to Julian; he was more stubborn than I gave him credit for. A second song started, then a third and a fourth. Traditional salsa music mixed with rock and pop, and I followed as best I could.

When I glanced at Julian, I could tell he'd reached his breaking point. He sat impatiently and stewed to himself. One final nudge would get him here, where he belonged.

The song morphed into a new one, another Santana collab. I recognized the Nickelback singer. The beat revved up, heavy and hot, and went on about dancing into the night.

"Ramp it up," I said, breathing heavily. "You'll get some possessive sex after this."

"Oh, I intend to." If he replied to my first or second statement, I wasn't sure. "So will you. Move with me when I pull you back."

"Okay." I sucked in a breath and looked around, finally catching sight of Henry looking like he'd just returned with Joseph. And as I watched Joseph gesture toward me and say things in Henry's ear, I recognized Joseph for the snake he was. This went beyond flirting and trying to get into our pants.

"Ready?" Noah raised a brow, and I focused on the music. I let it drown me for the moment. I nodded. "Make it hot, kid."

I smirked, and he yanked me to his chest. His hands on my hips, one of my hands at the back of his neck, and we moved damn well. He led me almost as perfectly as Henry did, our hips moving and speaking of sexual tension that wasn't there.

"We're good," I chuckled breathlessly.

"Fuck yeah, we are." He grinned, his chest heaving. "Can you see my boy?"

I could. He was moving in the corner of my eye. "On his way."

He nodded once and eased up. "Next time I wanna get him out on the floor, you'll be my partner in crime."

"Count me in." That was about all I had time to say before Julian tapped me on the shoulder.

"May I cut in?" he asked with a tight smile.

He was too fucking sweet. I released Noah, and wanting to ease the tension from the younger of the two, I gave Julian's cheek a smacking kiss. "All yours, hon."

The look in his eyes softened slightly, though it had nothing on when he was in Noah's arms. I smiled as they forgot everyone around them, and then I made my way out of the little crowd and aimed for Henry.

Seeing the brief flash of worry in his eyes fueled my anger toward Joseph. Who fucking knew what he'd been saying to Henry.

Over the past year, I'd gotten a better grasp on Henry's insecurities, and they were valid. We had a big age gap, and I worked in an industry that had broken up too many relationships. People didn't care about commitment anymore, and rumors of cheating and bullshit circulated more than news of weddings.

Henry had come a long fucking way, though. He believed me when I said I belonged to him, and damn if I was gonna let Joseph ruin that. Now, I couldn't help but wonder what he'd been telling Henry when he and I split after my first trip to LA. Had he tried to come between us? Had he agreed with Henry, who'd been so sure I would wake up one day and want more? At this point, it wouldn't surprise me.

I remembered when Henry told me about Joseph and Oliver, how they'd been in a weird relationship back in the day. He'd trusted Joseph's judgment when he shouldn't have; he listened to his friend.

"I see you're having fun," Joseph noted with a smile as I reached them. "I was just telling Henry how hot you and Noah were together."

"I have no fucking doubt you were telling him that." I shook my head and slipped my hand into Henry's. He was struggling with something, his jaw ticking with tension. I addressed Joseph again. "Did he tell you to step off and quit coming on to us?"

Joseph sighed and rolled his eyes. "You've gotten it all wrong, Zach. There's nothing bad about wanting to have fun."

"There is when those you wanna have fun with ain't fucking interested!" Holy shit, my anger exploded. "How motherfucking hypocritical can you be? After the shit you went through with your dad, you meet Henry and start an organization where kids without support can come to get away from harassment and abuse. You have pamphlets outside every goddamn office telling girls that it's okay to say no, but how many times do we have to tell *you*?"

He was taken aback by my outburst, eyes growing large, though he recovered too fast for my liking. "You can't possibly compare me to sexual predators. For God's sake, you need to take it down a notch."

"He's right, Joseph." Henry spoke with a low, barely controlled voice, and I couldn't make sense of his mood. Something was brewing, other than the storm nearby, and he seemed almost more pissed at himself. "Last time I came down to LA, Zach picked me up at the airport and said you'd invited him home for drinks after a shoot."

Joseph didn't wanna hear it. He scoffed and said we were blowing shit out of proportion.

I stared at him. Now that the issue was out in the open between all three of us, I wondered if there was something he wanted to say to me when Henry wasn't around. He'd hinted at some things before, just minor catty comments. Henry and I were "so different," he'd said. One time when we'd gone out after work, he'd made a remark about Henry's and my sex life. Apparently, it was a relief that I liked to bottom because Henry didn't do that. "I mean...I would know," he'd added with a wink.

I'd brushed it off. I wasn't gonna let him get to me, nor was I gonna tell him about something that wasn't any of his goddamn business.

"We're not interested in you," I said slowly, 'cause I was clearly speaking to a child. "I get that you're into Henry—"

"Excuse me?" he chuckled incredulously.

Henry sighed and released my hand to scrub his face.

It was one of those things not even Henry believed, but I saw it.

"Do you not see how young and naïve he is, Henry?" Joseph turned it around, and there it was. He couldn't have been clearer. He wanted us to break up. When he faced me again, he was a condescending prick. "Sweetie, I understand you come from a place where it's different. But where we're from, wanting to get someone into bed doesn't mean we're in love and want to settle down and have a family."

I smiled and scratched my nose. "Henry, can I have a moment with Joseph?"

Henry didn't like that at all. "That's not wise. I know the look on your face, and I have no desire to scrape Joseph off the ground later."

I lifted a brow at him. "You got your moment. Now I want mine. I'll be on my best behavior." I was pretty sure I could restrain myself. Sort of.

I was a grown man. Henry couldn't keep me from having words with Joseph, and he knew it.

"I'll get a drink," he muttered and walked away.

I faced Joseph and folded my arms over my chest. "You can be honest now. You want me gone, yeah?"

"Why would I want that?" He feigned disinterest and leaned against the wall. "Your days are already numbered."

"Oh, really. Why's that?"

Joseph chuckled. "I've known Henry far longer than you have. He'll grow bored with Washington and fret himself half to death wondering when you're gonna cheat on him. And you know what? It's because you don't make sense. He belongs in LA, and he should be with someone who's more compatible."

"Someone like you?" I cocked my head.

He gave me a sharp glare, and I knew I'd struck a nerve.

"I used to view you as a threat," I admitted. "Now I'm just watching you wreck everything you have with Henry. He's not interested, and every time you've flirted with me, you've disrespected your friend. You've *upset* him."

"He'll come around," he snapped, and his composure was gone. "He and I aren't perfect, but we make more sense than you do. He wouldn't have to worry with us. We've done this before. I'd make it good for—" He shut his mouth, anger boiling over but no more words tumbling out. His secret was out.

To my own surprise, I was calm. I hadn't imagined it. It wasn't in my head. His twisted love for Henry was right there.

I jabbed a finger into his chest. "The second you're not professional at work, I'll let Brooklyn know everything." He would be taken off the project in a heartbeat, I had no doubt. "From now on, we're done. That includes Henry, and I won't say it again."

"Good luck with that," he chuckled bitterly. "Henry and I have been friends for over ten years."

I didn't say anything else. I left his bitch ass behind and went to find Henry. He wasn't outside, so I tried inside the villa, where I eventually located him at the bar.

I slid onto the barstool next to his, feeling numb. I didn't like numbness. It left me clueless about how I would feel later on when I'd processed.

"Is he alive?" Henry lifted his whiskey glass and took a sip.

"I didn't even raise my voice." My mind went blank, and when the bartender came over, I said I didn't want anything. "What did you tell him when you went behind the building?"

"That we weren't interested." His voice grew quieter. "I don't understand how this got so out of hand. I'm disappointed in him —and I'm angry."

I had a feeling I was too; I just couldn't get a grasp on it. My knee bounced, and I glanced around us. The bar area was protected by a chest-high wall of plants and bronze statues, and I could only hear the dinner guests on the other side. People were having a great time. Music was playing.

My evening was ruined. *Fuck*. The bouncing got worse as trickles of fury seeped in.

Were Henry's issues gonna make a comeback now? Were *mine*? As rough as this year had been work-wise, we'd been doing so well. We made sure to communicate every worry, and as time went on, they had lessened. We'd built our foundation and trusted each other.

"When I left Malibu the first time, and you and I kinda broke up, did you talk to Joseph?"

Henry side-eyed me, frowning. "In general, or...?"

I shrugged, then nodded. "And about us. Did he say anything?"

He frowned some more, thinking back. "No, not really. He understood my fears... He may have mentioned he thought it was poor taste that you didn't."

I chuckled once. "Of course he did."

Henry's expression changed. He became careful and faced me better. "You're upset. What did he tell you?"

"That you and I don't make sense." Though, that wasn't what made my anger rise. At the same time, exhaustion flooded me, and I feared I wasn't just fighting against Joseph. What if Henry still had doubts? I could fight as long as it was him and me against the world. But if I had to start over and convince *Henry*... Christ.

"Can..." He trailed off and looked over his shoulder. "Let's talk outside, please."

Tired as fuck, I followed him out to the front of the villa. The poorly lit parking lot was on the side of the road, and Henry walked until we could have privacy.

The thunder was getting closer. The smell of rain lingered in the air.

"Talk to me, Zachary."

"Why did you look tense after I danced with Noah?" I blurted out.

He drew in a breath and started to speak but closed his mouth again. Next, he pinched the bridge of his nose. "I was angry with myself." His hand fell back to his side. "I stood there and listened to Joseph—well, you know what he said about you and Noah." Yeah, that we'd been hot together. "And it hit me, I suppose, that Joseph was being a lousy friend. And has been—for months and months. Something's changed, and I don't understand why I've let it go on."

That was infinitely better than I'd feared.

"More than that," he went on, "it pissed me off that I listened to him. It may have only lasted a minute or two, but I listened to him. I grew unsure, jealous, and doubtful, and I feel terrible about it because you've never done anything to deserve my doubt."

Okay. Okay, this was much better. We were human, and we couldn't help how we felt. This shit happened. "Has that minute or two passed?" I had to know. "Because I can face anything as long as you're there with me. I can't fight Joseph if part of you is on his side."

Henry stepped closer and cupped my cheek. "Darling, since the day I met you, you've been the only man whose side I've been on. You're the love of my life, and I trust you. That's why I was so angry, because I felt like I was betraying you by listening to him. I'm…" He closed his eyes briefly and released a breath. "I'm done with Joseph. He's not the man I became friends with, and he's crossed too many lines. Fuck—" He really was upset with himself. "I cannot believe I let his advances slide because of our history. He's been disrespectful to both of us."

I was about to kiss him, but Henry had other plans, mainly beating himself up.

"For chrissakes, when I first spotted you and Noah, I *smiled*." He took a step back and rubbed his jaw, visibly frustrated. "You were enjoying yourself, and you're so incredibly sexy when you laugh. I was happy—it filled me with this surge of pleasure because I know you value the friendships you've created with Noah and Julian, and then I let Joseph destroy it."

"For a minute or two," I reminded him. I couldn't let him take this too far. We were good now. That's what I wanted him to focus on. It'd only been a hiccup, and Joseph was on his way out of our lives. "Come back to me, Henry. We should focus on ending this night on a better note. Yeah?"

He sighed once more, slowly giving up on the fight, and the tension disappeared from his shoulders. "You're right again."

"Come here," I whispered. Drawing him close, I reached up and covered his mouth with mine, leaving brushing kisses until I felt him relaxing against me. "I love you."

"I love you too." He deepened the kiss, sweeping his tongue into my mouth with sensual strokes. "You have no idea how much."

I wanted to spend the rest of my life figuring it out. How was that for devotion?

The man better propose to me soon. I wanted his ring on my finger and to see mine on his.

I backed Henry up against the nearest car and squeezed his firm ass. Possessiveness mingled with the relief at not having to convince him we were perfect together. He knew like I did. It was us two, no one else. Henry seemed to catch on, putting up less of a fight to be in control, and I angled my head for a deeper kiss.

His surrender was always so fucking heady.

"Your ass is mine as soon as we get back to the hotel," I said, breathing heavily.

"Anything you want."

Good, because he owed me a dance first.

Five minutes later, I got what I wanted. Henry took control as we found ourselves in the middle of the back terrace with dancing couples surrounding us. We danced to slow songs and upbeat ones, never moving far away from each other. He guided me like a god and made me lose sight of everything that wasn't him.

The storm wasn't gonna miss Cancún at all. Thunder rolled in, and the first raindrop landed on my nose.

Henry pulled me close and brushed the drop away with his thumb. Our labored breaths mingled, and his gaze was so intense I couldn't break it.

I could get sappy when I wanted to, and though I didn't believe the eyes were the windows to our souls or whatever, I could see my future in his.

A slower song began, the enticing notes of the guitar trapping us in another rhythm. I slid my hand up to his neck, his skin hot and damp, and he hauled me flush against his body. Our lower bodies moved in tune with the music in unhurried figure-eight motions, making it impossible to stay unaffected.

"You're killing me." I grinned, breathless.

He brushed his nose to mine. "Quiet." The tip of his tongue flicked my upper lip, and I shuddered. At the same time, the rain picked up.

"But I'm hard—"

His swift kiss cut me off, and I took the command seriously this time.

As the rain morphed into a full-blown downpour, people started rushing inside.

Not us. The tension thickened with every heartbeat, and I groaned as he squeezed my ass. The heat was becoming unbearable. Rain clung to my eyelashes, and I blinked the drops away. Our clothes were bordering on soaked, and my need for him was one move away from turning into a frenzy.

Henry spun me around, then gripped my hip tightly and pulled me back. His mouth latched on to my neck, and he sucked lightly at the wet skin.

"Henry," I panted.

"I know, baby."

We had to get out of here.

CHAPTER 5

WE HAVE TRUST AND SLUTTERY

"I hate these situations," Brooklyn said bluntly. "What you did could've cost Rob his job, but because the results were so good, it's pointless to bitch about it."

"I understand." I shifted the phone from one ear to the other as Henry handed me my wallet. I tucked it into the back pocket of my cargo shorts. "I knew the risk, Brooklyn. I was also ready to take the fall for it."

"That doesn't matter, hon," she sighed. "Rob was responsible for your shoot yesterday. It reflects poorly on him if he can't stand up against a couple models."

"I think I'm insulted," I said halfheartedly. "Henry says I'm charming as fuck."

That earned me a what-am-I-going-to-do-with-you look from him.

I gave him my best smile.

To be honest, I was relieved. I'd witnessed Brooklyn tear into people, and when I woke up to Joseph's text about a breakfast meeting in his villa, I'd assumed it was related to my stunt with chucking the script.

"That's called bias," Brooklyn replied wryly, "but unfortunately, he's right. I skimmed through the footage, and you just became the comic relief that pokes fun at the company. People love that, and if they didn't love *you* already, they will now."

Okay, I'd just wanted to be myself, not some scripted version.

I felt better about going to this breakfast meeting now, though. I'd been cleared by the boss lady, and the man who wanted *my* man better keep things professional.

Brooklyn and I wrapped up the call, and Henry walked out onto our balcony, which struck me as odd.

"We gotta go, baby." I pocketed my phone and followed him.

He'd taken a seat in one of the two chairs, and the table between them had the paper, a cup of coffee, and his iPad.

"Breakfast's in five minutes." I frowned.

"Oh. I'm not going with you." He shed his tee, and I ogled his chest for a beat. I'd raked my fingers through his sparse chest hair hard enough to leave some marks. Hot. Wait, what was he saying? "I have a Skype breakfast with Martin, and I thought I'd check in with the pet sitter and the boys. And Ruth, of course."

Chatting with Nan had become an *of course* thing, evidently.

"So you're gonna let me face Joseph alone?" I asked.

He smiled and flipped open the paper. "I'm trusting you, darling. As far as I'm concerned, he's no longer part of our lives."

Sure, great, awesome, but I liked having Henry with me.

"I'm disgruntled," I decided.

He chuckled and peered closer at the balcony railing, probably estimating when the sun would reach him. He had another hour or so, I guessed. "You'll be fine. I figured I should enjoy some time off. I'll be here when you get back from work."

Well, fuck. He wasn't even tagging along to the shoot?

"You're gonna sit here all day?" And not be with me?

"No, I thought I'd go for a run later. I have to stay in shape." He patted his stomach, and I rolled my eyes. I was the lazy one in our relationship, yet he had this obsession with exercising and eating well because he thought he'd fall behind if he didn't.

There wasn't a whole lot to keep up with, that was all.

"All right…" I realized I was being childish, and I didn't care. "I guess I'll go, then."

"Without giving me a kiss?" He lifted a brow.

"Well, no." I was so whipped for him.

The breakfast meeting was nothing but a way for Joseph to assert his authority. He reprimanded me in front of the others for going off-script, and I let him have his little moment. I did mention I'd talked to Brooklyn and that she liked the result, after which Joseph said stiffly, "Yes, well, you're sticking to the program now."

I had no intention of doing otherwise.

With that out of the way, we were once again whisked away for filming, and Joseph had decided to work on my team today. He'd also decided to host a dinner at his villa tonight, and everyone was required to attend.

I was paired with Maliah, so Noah was with us.

"Where's Julian?" I asked.

He took a sip of his coffee. "He wanted to do some Christmas shopping. Think he was asking Henry to join him for lunch, too."

"Ah. Cool." I stifled a yawn.

Today's work was gonna be mentally easy and physically taxing. We arrived at a beach that was famous for its caves and rock formations, and basically, all I was going to do was execute dives and swim underwater. We were filming inserts that would be added to the videos, so there was no talking or anything.

The crew was bigger today, including two guys on a boat and one beefy dude playing security detail. It was mostly to keep vacationers away from being in the shot.

No makeup for me today, which suited me perfectly. Instead, I got to chill with Noah for an hour while Joseph got Maliah ready.

Paulie was putting on scuba gear to film us underwater, and another cameraman was gonna film us from above.

I relaxed back in my director's chair and listened with one ear as Noah talked about the lighting. I supposed being an actual Hollywood director, he'd have opinions on a low-budget set like this one. Or maybe it wasn't low-budget, but there was very little direction involved.

"Hey, Joseph!" Noah hollered. The man in question was standing some twenty feet away, waterproofing Maliah's makeup. "You guys might wanna hurry up. The rocks over there will shield your diving spot from the sunlight within the hour."

I snickered at his anal-retentiveness.

Joseph squinted, holding a hand up for the sun. "Does that matter?"

Noah shrugged and leaned back in his own chair. "With videos titled *Never Shadowed* and *A Day in the Light*, you tell me. But that's none of my business."

"Oh God," I laughed. "There's a Kermit meme out there with your name on it."

He winked.

"Okay, let's get started, everyone!" Joseph felt the urgency suddenly, and he gave Maliah a last touch-up on her bronzed cheekbones. "Zach and Maliah, we'll do half a dozen dives and go from there."

"Jesus," Noah muttered under his breath. "That makes no sense. Unless he's gonna haul out a hairdryer and fix Maliah's hair before every dive, the first take won't matter if you don't nail it."

I'll give him that one. We could only go from dry to wet once.

I got up from my chair and tightened the drawstrings to my standard black trunks.

Time to dive.

I was exhausted and slightly sunburned when we returned to the resort.

Henry was in a good mood.

I crash-landed facedown on our bed.

"And Tyler's professor used his work as an example in a workshop, so he was happy," Henry went on, giving me a recounting of his day. "Hmm…what else…oh, Martin says hello. He dealt with your agent, and I told him you don't need a new one since you'll only be taking work from Brooklyn."

"Okay…great…" I yawned into the pillow and didn't move as Henry began pulling down my shorts.

"I had lunch with Julian," he mentioned. "We went to a lovely place that served the best tempura shrimp I've had in a long time." He removed my flip-flops, then rid me of my shorts and underwear. "Which reminds me. We have a connection in LA on the way home, so I told Martin we'd go out for sushi."

"*Umph*…all right. You know what I like." Fuck, I was tired.

"I'll make sure they have spicy tuna, baby boy," he promised and smacked my ass. "You go take a shower. Julian told me we have dinner at Joseph's."

"Can't we just fuck and nap?"

"No, you can look alive and go take your shower."

I didn't whine or nothin'.

The showering and getting dressed for dinner took twenty minutes, and Henry picked up the conversation as if there hadn't been a break when I exited the bathroom.

"Ty told me he's a little concerned about Mattie."

That made me look up from zipping my shorts. "Why, what's wrong?"

Henry picked out a new shirt for me. Apparently, my button-down was wrong. I smiled when he handed me a tee, one that said "His Personal Fluffer." It was one of my favorites, and he was specific about when I could wear it because it embarrassed him sometimes. For instance, I wasn't allowed to wear it when seeing

Nan. He thought it was entirely inappropriate. I just loved it when he got that invisible flush, his expression screaming of self-consciousness but lacking the actual blush.

"He's not sure," he replied pensively. "It could be nothing, but Tyler wonders about Mattie's new friends. He's out late and is often tired."

I nodded slowly and changed clothes. "We'll talk to him. I can call him tomorrow." Though, having heard he was tired more than once now, it could be a conversation best had in person.

Akira and Noah found my T-shirt hilarious, and my mood had brightened after sneaking a quick attack on Henry before we left our suite. I hadn't given him much choice, to be fair. He'd been coming out of the shower when I'd stolen his towel and sunk to my knees. By the time he'd wanted to come, I'd spun him to face the counter and bent him over so I could tongue-fuck his ass until he shot his load. A rim job *always* got him where I wanted him when I was the top. And now, he was my sweetheart.

Dinner was served both on the modest terrace and in the living room. A buffet of sorts, consisting of appetizers and delicious carbs, was set up on a table inside the sliding doors, while the barbecue area was stocked with skewers, grilled chicken, steak, and burgers.

"Save us some good seats, love." I kissed Henry's jaw. "I'll get us food."

While he found seats on one of the couches, I went outside and filled two plates with everything that looked amazing. So... everything. The sound of Joseph's laughter rang above the dinner conversation, and I looked over my shoulder to see him chatting up one of the assistants. Someone was looking to get laid.

My one goal was to avoid him as much as possible and enjoy myself tonight, so I returned back inside and added to the mountain of food. Maliah and I trailed the length of the buffet table together.

"Is it just me or does Joseph want us to see how nice his villa is?" she wondered.

"It's not just you," I laughed under my breath. The way I saw it, this dinner was no different from the breakfast meeting. Here, he was the star of the show. The work crew who made less money sucked up to him; it was how the entertainment industry worked. You sussed out the person with a better position, and you kissed ass.

Joseph needed an ego boost.

After dumping a selection of dipping sauces on the plates, I made my way to where Henry was talking to Noah. There was a mention of vegetarian lasagna, and it was all I needed to hear to zone out.

"Thank you, darling." Henry accepted his plate. "Noah's going to send me his recipe for vegetarian—"

"Yeah, I love meat," I said. "Red meat, white meat, man meat, and whatever you call fish meat."

Julian snickered.

"Hey." Noah nudged Julian. "You love my lasagna."

"True," Julian conceded. "It's still funny."

Noah smirked and shook his head, then refocused on me. "Tell us more about this man meat you love."

I rested my plate on my thigh and pointed to my T-shirt. "I'm lucky enough to be his fluffer. His name is Henry Jonathan Bennington, and he's about eight or nine inch—"

"*Zachary.*" Henry stared at me, half horrified, and I guffawed like a loon.

"I haven't even gotten to the girth yet!" I protested. Noah and Julian cracked up at my silliness—and possibly at Henry's expression. Ruffling his feathers was just too funny. For as filthy as he was in the bedroom, he was a real proper gentleman in public. "Oh God, I'm Martin," I realized with a laugh. "First time he and

Henry invited me for brunch, Martin was demonstrating the size of his hookup's dick."

"We clearly hang out with the wrong gays," Noah joked.

"And you blushed then," Henry told me, still affronted. "Now look at you."

I shrugged and grinned. "I guess, like Maliah, I learn from the best. I'm a power slut for you, man."

"That's priceless," Julian laughed.

I finally got Henry to crack a smile, even as he tried really hard not to.

"I think that may have been the sweetest thing I've ever said." I bit into a piece of buffalo chicken and licked some sauce off the corner of my mouth. "I need that printed on a T-shirt."

"Are you high, Zach?" Noah chuckled.

"No, I'm in love, dude!" I exclaimed. "This chicken is really good too."

Henry let out an affectionate laugh.

"Anyway." I waved a hand. "Enough about my sluttitude. Anyone up for some Christmas shopping tomorrow?"

CHAPTER 6

HA-HA, HENRY'S HIGH

*J*oseph probably didn't anticipate that his dinner would turn into a party. It just happened naturally when you invited LA people who smoked weed for every meal except brunch. We didn't mess with brunch. Brunch was sacred.

By ten thirty, music was pouring out of the villa, and Akira and Tyrese were jumping into the hot tub. Room service delivered alcohol that was gonna set Joseph back a pretty penny, and Julian, of all people, was the weed connection. I knew he smoked on rare occasions, but it was just one of those things that didn't really add up when you met him. He was soft-spoken and sweet, saving the unrestricted humor for when he was truly comfortable. Or when he was getting high, evidently.

Noah took a quick break to be a disciplinarian and escort Maliah back to her suite.

"What're you waiting for, Zach?" Akira yelled from the terrace.

"Henry!" I gave her a *duh* expression. Henry was in the bathroom, and I wasn't getting in that tub without him.

In the meantime, I took control of the music and changed it

to something better than classic rock. We needed club remixes for this. Then I made myself a huge Violet Haze to drink, and Henry got a Tequila Sunrise.

When my man finally returned, we headed out to the terrace and set our drinks on the edge of the Jacuzzi.

"Are you guys naked in there?" I peered into the water, as if I could see past the bubbles. "I don't wanna scare anyone with my nakedness if you brought swimsuits."

If there was one thing I'd lost in my year as a model, it was my modesty. For the most part.

"Oh, just drop your panties," Akira huffed. Raising herself up slightly, she made it perfectly clear she wasn't wearing a bikini top. Fair enough. "We wanna see what the fluffer bragged about earlier."

I laughed, whereas Henry abruptly stopped unzipping his shorts.

"I will fucking punish you, Zachary," he told me.

I puckered my lips in a kiss, then shed my clothes and got in. *Oh God, yes.* The hot water was perfect. Kinda like my evening so far. And speaking of punishments to improve my night further... Given his current, hot-as-fuck bottom mood, the only one who had to worry about punishments was him.

"Don't forget to give us a show." I winked and took a sip of my drink.

He narrowed his eyes at me, only to give up and mutter something about "youngsters these days." He wasn't a particularly modest man either, so he got rid of his clothes and merely sighed and shook his head at Akira's catcalling.

I made room for him, wanting to sit on his lap and snuggle. "Who are you kidding, Henry?" I murmured in his ear, and I sat down sideways across his thighs. "You love your youngster. Especially, you know, when he's a pain in your ass."

His eyes danced with silent laughter at my pun, and he didn't deny it. And because he was a natural-born ass addict, he slipped a hand under me and circled my asshole with a finger.

"Behave." I suppressed a shiver.

"I can't help it." He circled my opening a few more times before pushing a digit inside.

Jesus. I cleared my throat. "Here. I got you a Tequila Sunrise." I handed him his drink.

"I saw that," he chuckled. "You know what tequila does to me, though."

I didn't want the warning. I wanted the results. Henry drunk on tequila was intoxicating—and totally worth taking care of his intense hangover.

"Room for one more?" Oh joy, Joseph was joining us.

"And us." That was better. Julian showed up with Noah, who was already tossing his clothes on the ground. "I bring pot."

"My hero," Akira sang. "Now I just need Hallie." She spoke of her girlfriend. "This tub is turning into a sausage fest."

I laughed and nearly choked on my drink. "We can talk some more about your tits if you think that evens the score a bit."

She *loved* to talk about those.

For emphasis, she cupped her ladies and blew me a kiss.

"I think the only one here who hasn't touched them is Henry."

Henry hummed but was too busy finger-fucking me to respond.

"And us," Julian repeated. He was blushing as he got into the tub, and Noah positioned him like Henry had me. I was happy to have them between us and Joseph.

"So much hotness around." I waggled my eyebrows at Noah and Julian and shifted on Henry's lap. Catching Akira's huff, I humored her. "Yes, sure, even you, girl."

"You guys are fucking nuts," Tyrese said with a rich chuckle.

"When did you touch Akira's breasts?" Henry asked, confused.

I scratched my nose, thinking back on the exact occasion. It was a shoot. "The Christmas campaign last year, right?"

Akira nodded. "One of the bolder shots. Zach's hands were my bra."

"That was a good one," Tyrese noted. "First time I thought the makeup on a dude was actually hot."

I'd gotten good publicity for that shoot, I remembered. There was a lot of black and gold going on.

"Ah, now I remember," Henry said. "You were incredibly sexy." He kissed my jaw and stroked me high up on my thigh.

If I got hard in the tub, I'd end up doing something that wasn't fit for public consumption, so I nudged Henry's hand away from my butt.

"That was when Brooklyn made me the head of makeup." Joseph's comment sounded too much like bragging than a casual recollection. I snorted and sipped more of my drink.

"Guys...?" Julian offered the joint to anyone who wanted.

To my surprise, it was Henry who spoke up. "Oh, it's been decades. I shouldn't." He looked tempted.

I grinned, always happy to learn new things about my man. "Let's discuss this," I said for only him to hear, and I accepted the joint and took a brief pull from it. "I wanna know how you got high while I was still in diapers."

"What're you two whispering about?" Akira demanded.

"Zach's being a dirty little boy," Henry drawled. I smiled widely, took another hit, then handed it to him. As he inhaled from it, I slowly let out the sweet smoke. "Is Mexico still bad?"

I shook my head no. I was having a great time, but that didn't mean I wasn't excited to go home.

Eventually, Akira's girlfriend arrived, and we drank and smoked and laughed at bad jokes until we were hoarse. Henry was high enough to be able to admit he was curious about Akira's transition to become who she was. He asked about her surgery and journey in general. And Akira being Akira when she was drunk, she made it about her rack. On a day off, she worked hard to raise awareness about transgender people. On a night off, she was all, "But check out my boobs!" She was adorable.

My shoulders shook with laughter as she swam closer to us so Henry could touch her tits.

"They're softer than I expected," he mused.

"And your hand is kinda amazing," Akira said frankly, taking a puff from a new joint.

Henry removed his hand. "Jesus. Imagine Martin's face when I tell him I went to Cancún and fondled a woman."

Noah and I guffawed at that, before Julian declared it was "his turn." That spoke volumes about how high he was.

"I'm gonna tease you relentlessly about this tomorrow," Noah murmured and nuzzled Julian's neck. In response, Julian sucked in a breath and grew rigid, but I was pretty sure it wasn't for what Noah had *said*...as much as what Noah might be doing underwater.

The thought sent a lazy thrill down my spine, rocking through me slowly, so fucking thoroughly. I tilted my head at Henry as he finished his drink, and the second he set down the glass, I leaned in and kissed him.

He smiled into the kiss, his hands rubbing my thigh and lower back.

"Don't you have a hotel room for that?" Joseph asked tightly.

I broke the kiss and looked over at Noah and Julian—wait. What? Oh, that was rich. Noah and Julian were possibly *fucking*, and Joseph was chastising Henry and me for kissing?

Joseph, sweetie, your jealousy is showing.

I chuckled at the underlying anger in Joseph's eyes before I stole another kiss from Henry. "Come on, hon. Let's go." Probably best we got a move on while I wasn't yet indecently hard.

Henry followed me out of the Jacuzzi, and I wrestled my way back into my clothes. The pot was preventing me from getting hotheaded, and Joseph could consider himself lucky for that.

"Christ," I snickered, seeing Henry struggling with his pants.

Stepping closer, I steadied him and kissed his lazy grin, then helped him with the buttons. "How much did you smoke?"

"Too much for my age," he whispered. "I'm high, darling."

I laughed. "You're cute as fuck too."

The others, besides Joseph, were too busy with their own romances to care we were leaving the party, so we returned inside without anyone mentioning anything.

The music was louder in the living room, and everyone was drunk off their ass. Henry snuck up behind me and pressed his mouth to my neck, quickly derailing my thoughts. Maybe we didn't have to go back to our suite yet...

"I want you," he muttered in my ear. "I've suffered all night, having you on my lap."

I shuddered and turned in his arms. "Wanna stay and dance and drink for a while?"

He shook his head and kissed me hard, parting my lips with a swipe of his tongue. "I want to fuck. Don't deny me."

Lust bolted through me, causing my head to swim. One look at his handsome face and the sheer need in his eyes was enough to surrender, but I was gonna take that control back. I wanted him to beg.

I ghosted my knuckles over his scruffy cheek. "You're acting like a whore."

He lowered his gaze and flushed, only to take another kiss so hard and passionate that I lost my footing.

"You can take me in the bathroom," he suggested under his breath.

I groaned and deepened the kiss. I had a better idea than the bathroom, though. And call me a prick, but I didn't care. Pushing my man through the party crowd, I guided him backward to Joseph's bedroom.

"I may be high, but I'm pretty sure," Henry said, breathing heavily, "this is petty."

I closed the door behind us, and the music faded to a muted thudding.

"Do you care?" I unbuttoned his shirt and started kissing his chest.

"Not one bit—Jesus Christ." He hissed when I grazed my teeth around a nipple and sucked lightly on it. "Do whatever you want with me."

His words went straight to my cock. Joseph's bedroom was next to the living room, meaning the two areas shared the same view of the patio. I wanted Henry up against those glass doors, my cock drilling into him, while the others were mere feet away, enjoying the party in the hot tub.

"Unzip me." I kissed him hungrily and began backing him up toward the doors. "Feel how hard you make me?"

"Yes," he whispered, wrapping his fingers around my dick. He shuddered and looked down between us as I spread my hands over his chest and kissed his neck. "I could watch your cock for hours. I love touching it."

"It's about to fuck you." I nipped at his chin and smiled at his sharp intake of air. "Hands on the glass, baby."

While he undid his pants and turned around, I retrieved a single packet of lube from my wallet and coated my cock. Wanting to savor the moment before he stunned me right back into being his slut, I decided to push him deeper into his mindset. I sank to my knees behind him and squeezed his firm ass, spreading the cheeks to expose him to me.

"Oh hell, not again." He hung his head and moaned. "You've already got me going crazy, Zachary. I can't take—" He could take it, and he gasped as I leaned in and licked his hole softly. "Jesus fuck."

I teased him mercilessly with soft and unhurried tongue kisses. Whenever I entered him, he clenched down and breathed harder. But I wanted more. I wanted the shameless pleas.

"Who does this sexy ass belong to?" I pushed two fingers inside and licked around them. I caught the movement of his right hand, letting me know he was stroking himself. "Go on. Tell me, Henry."

"You—only you. Fuck me now." He grunted and trembled. "God, Zach. Please fuck me."

And I couldn't fucking resist. I'd make him beg properly before he got off, though. I rose off the floor and jacked my slick cock, then inched closer and let him feel me. I slid the head of me between his cheeks and rubbed him until he was pushing back in an attempt to get more.

"*Zachary.*" His voice was laced with impatience.

"That's not the magic word." I slapped my hand to one of his cheeks and squeezed roughly, my fingers digging in. "Did you forget?"

He hung his head again and breathed deeply. "Please. Please push your perfect cock inside me."

"Mm, much better." I forced myself inside slowly. "God." A breath gusted out of me. "You're always so tight." With a firm grip on his hips, I withdrew and pushed in again. I couldn't tear my eyes away. "Fuck yourself on me. Show me how much you want it."

He kept one hand on the glass, the other on his dick, and pushed back carefully. He was there, I could sense it, in that mind-set where he tested the waters. Possessiveness flooded my senses, turning my touches into reassuring caresses. I wanted to take care of him.

"Amazing," he breathed.

"You can go harder, love." I slipped a hand under his open shirt and rubbed his back. "Do you do those exercises you told me about?" There were few things I loved more than making sex mind-blowing for him, so when he'd told me to train my muscles, I'd started and never stopped. It wasn't only women who did Kegels. "Do you keep yourself this tight for my sake?"

"Of course I do." Goose bumps appeared where my hand

touched him, and he met my next thrust with more force. "I want it to be good for you."

I cursed and swallowed the rush of lust, gaze zeroing in on every inch he took of me. He'd made me do it in front of him once. The clenching. It'd been one of the hottest experiences ever, and I wasn't gonna miss out.

"You'll show me sometime." I reached down and cupped my balls as he eased away. "I'll have you on all fours like you did with me, and I'll watch you do them. And I'll come...right here." I slid a finger along his crease.

He let out a groan that caused me to lose my composure. Gripping his hips again, I shoved my cock deep and planted my forehead between his shoulder blades. It was only the beginning, and I started fucking him like my body demanded. In long, deep thrusts, I pushed him closer to the glass doors, and his sexy sounds grew urgent and heavy.

"Fuck, you feel incredible," I grunted.

My body flushed with heat, and everything around us disappeared. Henry finally got to begging—begging me to fuck him harder, deeper, faster, because he wanted to feel it afterward. He wanted the ache and the soreness to remind him how I'd taken him.

"That's not all you'll feel," I promised huskily. "I won't let you clean up after this." I sucked in a sharp breath as he clenched down on me. "You can thank your lucky stars your pants are black, 'cause you'll walk around with my come inside you."

"Oh God," he groaned. "It won't work. I'll feel it down my legs."

"*Good.*" I gnashed my teeth together, speeding up. The chase was on, and I lost myself in the swirls of pleasure that raged inside me. "You know you love it. It drives you fucking crazy when your little boy uses your ass like this. Doesn't it?"

He moaned unintelligibly.

The click of a door broke through my haze, albeit weakly. I

shoved my cock deep and lazily dragged my hooded gaze toward the door behind me. *Motherfucker.* I didn't stop fucking Henry, who clearly hadn't noticed our visitor. Joseph stood there, fucking gaping. Jaw dropped, shock written across his face.

My mouth twisted into a dark smirk. The thrill turned me into a gloating bastard, I guess. 'Cause fuck that motherfucker. I merely faced my man again, murmured how good he felt around my cock, how I couldn't fucking wait to empty myself inside his ass, and how much I loved him.

"*Fuck*, close," he growled. "More, darling. *Please take me—*"

I rammed in, effectively stealing his breath. The euphoria nearly blinded me, and I barely registered the second click of the door. One quick glance told me we were alone again, and I shuddered, finding my focus once more. I took in the sounds, the heady scent of us, the slick push and pull, and the sensations erupting.

I came with a breathless, gritty warning. I rocked into him jerkily, out of control, and bit out a curse when he lost it too. His muscles tightened impossibly around me as he released in bursts, and I managed to fuck him through our orgasms.

He painted the glass door with his release.

Joseph could have it.

"Oh my God…" I rolled over and threw the covers over my head. "You've got to be *kidding* me, Henry."

How was this even possible? He'd been so fucked last night, and now he was letting the sun come in at hell-no o'clock.

"Let's have breakfast." The bed shifted with his weight, and he yanked away the covers to plant a kiss between my shoulder blades. "I'm showered, ready to go, and starving."

"This isn't happening." I buried my face in the pillow. "How are you not hungover?"

"I don't know," he mused. "The only pain I woke up with was a delicious one in my ass."

Yeah, well. The pain I woke up with was my boyfriend.

"I'm dying," I groaned. My head was killing me, as if there was a flock of woodpeckers trying to peck their way out of my skull. With hammers.

To make matters worse, my phone rang. Somewhere.

"I'll get it for you." Henry left the bed and located the offending object, answering it. "Zach's phone, Henry speaking." There was a slight pause. "Good morning, dear. Yes, he's—what?"

Lifting my head, I cracked an eye open to check the time. And I wanted to kick him in the fucking shin! It was seven forty-five. I didn't have a shoot until after lunch.

"Oh my." Henry sat down on the edge of the bed, his hand going to my shoulder. "Well, sure. I'm shocked, to be honest."

I sighed and figured I wouldn't be getting any more sleep. Might as well get up.

"I'll let him know," Henry said. "You too, Brooklyn. Goodbye." He ended the call and landed a hand on my buttocks. "You'll never believe this, Zach. Joseph quit his job."

Holy shit.

CHAPTER 7

I'M GONNA SAY IT, I'M GONNA SAY IT

"You could let me say it *once*," I pointed out.

"I could," he agreed. He turned the page in the LA Times and adjusted his glasses. A flight attendant walked past and offered us drinks, so I got a glass of bubbly, and Henry ordered a Bailey's with his coffee.

"Are you gonna?"

His mouth twitched, but he didn't look away from the paper. "Technically, you can say it however much you please, dear."

Uh, not when he'd threatened me with orgasm denial. What the fuck was that, anyway?

After another four days in Mexico, not an ounce of Henry was in the mood to play bottom or be "sweet and obedient," as he called me sometimes. To be honest, I fucking loved the brief period when he surged back and was extra bossy, but right now, I *really* wanted to say something. And he wasn't having it, partly because he found it juvenile, mostly because he liked to mess with me.

Weighing the options to myself, I looked out the window, stretched out my legs, and sipped my drink. We'd be landing in another hour, and if four days of trying to bargain hadn't worked, I wasn't gonna succeed before we got to LA.

I let it go for now.

We took a cab to our house in Santa Monica, the difference between the places we lived in never ceasing to amaze me. Back home, we had this massive home—by my standards, anyway—and here we had a fairly modest three-bedroom house with an outrageous price tag.

Henry had fallen for the cozy backyard with grapevines over the porch and the trees against the wooden fence, and I had fallen for it because of how he fell for it. Mornings of having breakfast out there, Henry picking lemons, figs, and the rare avocado ranked high up on my list of favorites.

Mattie and Ty ran the second floor. As long as shit didn't smell, Henry and I rarely ventured up there. The boys weren't home now, so we left our luggage in the hallway, shared a shower, then got dressed and ready for dinner with Martin.

"The place is surprisingly clean, isn't it?" Henry commented, rounding the kitchen island. He swiped a hand along the thick oak counter. "Do you think they hired a cleaning service?"

"See, this is why you shouldn't give them too much money," I said.

He lifted a brow. "If our biggest problem is two college kids spending money on cleaning, we could be worse off."

My mouth twisted. Okay, he had me there.

"Fine," I conceded. "We have twenty-four hours. Let's make the most of it."

"If by *the most of it,* you mean avoid people, I'm all for it," he chuckled.

"God yes, I'm exhausted." I crammed my wallet down into my skinny jeans and pushed up the sleeves of my button-down. The sushi place Martin had made reservations for was upscale, so no funny tees for me. "I want takeout tomorrow."

I'd asked Henry to change our flight home, so we had all of tomorrow and then our flight was at seven in the morning the day after. It should give us enough time to talk to Mattie and see what was going on with him.

"Benny's Tacos?" Henry suggested, handing me my leather jacket.

"*Yes.* Shrimp quesadilla." I donned the jacket, knowing what it did to him when I wore it. He had a James Dean fetish, I was pretty sure. "And ice cream from that place in Venice."

He approved. "Salt and Straw."

I nodded. They had the best flavors. Violet was only one of them.

We took Henry's car up to Hollywood, which took a fucking eternity, but I was in a good mood. We hadn't lost too much time —just a week. In less than thirty-six hours, we'd be back home in Westslope.

"You're wearing the cuff links I got you." I smiled and fingered the onyx studs. They were fancy, I thought, but just silly enough because I'd had "Z&H" engraved in the shiny surface.

"Of course." He clasped my hand and kissed my fingertips, and as sweet as he was, I couldn't.

"Safeword!" I yanked my hand free. "Not in these hills. Christ on a dick-stick." This was why I didn't drive in Hollywood. The winding roads needed to be ranked just like ski slopes.

Henry laughed. "You don't say *safeword*."

"Whatever. You know what I mean."

Watching light bondage porn with Henry had taught me a thing or two. I was hugely relieved his desires didn't go beyond keeping things spicy and red-hot in the bedroom, 'cause some of the BDSM stuff terrified me. But yeah, checking out that kind of porn with my man while he railed me hard from behind...? My pants got tighter at the thought.

"You'd tell me if you wanted to use whips and shit, right?" I scratched the side of my head.

He tossed me an incredulous look. "What on earth brought that on?"

I lifted a shoulder. "Just checking."

He chuckled and shook his head. "I assure you, no whips or anything of the sort."

"But maybe a new toy for Christmas." I threw that out there. "Like a vibrating cock ring or, or, or a prostate massager."

At that, Henry cleared his throat and adjusted his junk. "That can be arranged. I'll try anything that's about pleasure."

Unable to help myself, I reached across the middle and cupped his junk. "You'll teach me?"

He exhaled and made a turn up a steep road. "You seem to think I sit on a wealth of knowledge about these things."

"You're more experienced than me." I fondled his cock slowly as he thickened, and I rolled his balls in my hand. Kinda made me curse his dress pants.

"You're the first man I've explored with at this level." His voice came out huskier. "I've had my share of partners, but you can't compare what I've had before with the love of my life." He released the wheel to grab my hand and give it another kiss. "When comfort and trust are established...and our chemistry...? I can't describe what it's done to me. What *you* have done to me." Then he sadly placed my hand on his leg instead. "You respond to me so well, Zachary. So when I tell you to stop distracting me before I have to punish you, I know you'll obey me. Yes?"

My face burned, and I swallowed and nodded. "Yeah."

"Good boy."

Hnnghh.

We arrived at Yamashiro at a little before eight, and we stepped out of the car so the valet could take over, then walked hand in hand up to the restaurant that looked like it belonged in Japan.

Martin was waiting for us in the lobby, and I grinned when I saw him.

"It's been too damn long," he said dramatically. "Get over here, Zach."

"It's been less than two weeks." I laughed and hugged him, and I even agreed with him—this time. Two or three weeks were usually nothing 'cause we texted and talked on the phone. This month, he'd been beyond busy with his company. "How was the opening in MDR?"

Henry told me Martin had opened a new pastry shop in Marina del Rey yesterday, something that was becoming the norm. His franchise was expanding quickly, and it'd already gone out of state. There was one location in Portland and one in New York.

"I'm practically famous," he exclaimed. After exchanging a kiss on the cheek with Henry, he addressed the hostess and requested a table with a view. On the way, he filled us in more about the opening, and he couldn't resist throwing us a dig. "If only your lumberjack town were bigger and appreciated edible art," he sighed. "But, no. You insist on living like savages up there."

"Savages," I mouthed, exchanging a look with Henry.

He laughed silently.

We were shown to a table with a spectacular overlook of Los Angeles. The expansive view sparkled in the night and stretched out for miles over the city.

We placed our orders and talked more about Martin's business until our drinks arrived. I was happy things were going so well for him, and I hoped his plans to open a shop in Seattle came to fruition.

"Enough about me," Martin declared. "What the hell is this I hear about Joseph?"

I whipped my head to Henry. "Can I *please* just fucking say it? *Once?*"

"*No,*" he chuckled.

Goddammit. I slumped back in my seat and took a swig of my beer.

Henry faced Martin. "Joseph quit ShadowLight. I'm not sure what you've heard."

"Well, he called me," Martin replied. "He was drunk off his ass, but from what I understand, he wanted to transfer immediately." In other words, Joseph didn't wanna work on the campaign I was on. "He stated it was a personal issue, and Brooklyn couldn't do that with a snap of her fingers. So he said he'd quit if he couldn't change to another project."

"And there's no way Brooklyn would let herself be played." Henry poured sake for himself and Martin. "That's essentially the gist. He up and left, and we haven't heard from him since."

"You forgot the part where I'm the reason." I grinned.

"Oh, do tell." Martin gave me his full attention.

I leaned forward a bit. "Joseph's in love with Henr—"

"I knew it!" Martin said, and at the same time, Henry sighed, "Not this again—wait."

"Huh?" I looked to him.

He was frowning at Martin. "You *knew* it? What's that supposed to mean?"

"Oh, come on now, Felix." Martin waved a hand. "It's been obvious for years."

Henry was affronted. "First of all, you're Felix—I'm Oscar. Second of all, you're out of your mind."

"Ha!" Martin scoffed. "There's too much stick up your ass for you to be Oscar—"

"Actually, it's two against one," I said, "and no one cares which one of you is a fictional character and who's the other. You're both nitpicking princesses."

Martin eyed me, then Henry. And pointed at me. "He's all grown up."

Henry smiled. "I know, he's adorable."

"I give up." I threw up my hands before slumping back again and nursing my beer.

"Darling, try this sake." Henry extended his little cup. "It's not too dry, I promise."

I stared at him. Seriously. What the hell. He and Martin—I would never get used to how they functioned. It frustrated me as much as I craved it. The topic wasn't resolved in my opinion, yet now we'd moved on to wine made from rice.

"Anyway..." I twirled a finger to circle back to the subject, and I faced Martin. "What I haven't told *Felix* here is that I was fucking Henry in Joseph's bedroom in Cancún, and he was too busy begging and moaning my name to notice Joseph in the doorway."

Yeah, Henry wasn't thinking about the sake too much now. He was floored and speechless.

Martin legit applauded. "This is making my night. Tell me more."

"He came into the room?" Henry finally found his voice.

I inclined my head. "Thing is, when we were at that cantina, Joseph admitted he believed you and he made more sense as a couple than you and I do. I'm not talking outta my ass when I say he's into you. The fucker confirmed it, and I'm not gonna apologize for staking my claim."

"Delicious," Martin purred.

"I..." Henry didn't know what to say. "Christ. I had no idea."

I shrugged. That was my man in a chastity device—or nutshell. He didn't see his own appeal the way so many others did, so it was unthinkable that Joseph wanted more with him.

"Back to those characters," I said. "When did—"

"Yes, he's earned the Oscar label for a night." Martin nodded solemnly, having no clue where I was going with this. "I'm happy to hear you're so passionate in the sack, Henry. I thought for certain you'd be more uptight."

"He's tight, all right." I pretended to be Italian and kissed my fingertips. "In-fucking-credible."

Martin laughed heartily while Henry finished his sake in one go.

After dinner, we made plans to meet up in Seattle for Christmas shopping on the twenty-first. Martin claimed he needed a "transition city" and couldn't go straight from LA life to Heathenville in Camassia. Henry and I humored him, and then we said goodbye for now.

Across the street from the restaurant was a Japanese garden that shared the view we'd had inside, and Henry and I walked down the steps to enjoy a little peace and quiet. That feeling was hard to come by in this town, and we tended to savor it in whatever nook we found it.

Spotlights illuminated a few bonsai trees here and there, otherwise leaving the garden blanketed in complete darkness. I paused by a koi pond, peering into the water.

"Come here." Henry squeezed my hand and guided me over to a private spot. There, he positioned me in front of him, his hands gripping the wooden railing on either side of me. With his chin resting on my shoulder, I let out a sigh of contentment and looked out over the city.

It was so quiet and perfect. Moments like these had the best effect on me, tension draining away, my mind powering down. I placed his hands on my stomach instead, wanting his arms around me.

"Tonight was nice," he murmured.

I hummed, definitely agreeing. My gaze landed on the skyscrapers in downtown LA. "My brain is so hooked on this." I smiled lazily at his quiet chuckle, and I closed my eyes and brushed my hand over his. In the V between his thumb and index finger, his skin was the softest.

It was the same in the crease behind his knees and where his thigh met his crotch. The softest and smoothest skin that I could kiss and nuzzle for hours. He'd turned me into a freakishly cuddly person, and it was a hobby to explore and get to know every inch.

"I love you."

My mouth stretched into a smile. "I love you too."

He pressed a kiss to my neck, and then his warmth disappeared from my back. I frowned and opened my eyes, ready to demand he return my support pillar to me. Instead, he cut me off with a languid kiss. I angled my head as he cupped the back of my neck, and I stroked my tongue along his.

With a few chaste pecks, he broke the connection. And went down on one knee. *Holy fuck.* The rush of emotions tightened my gut and made me react weirdly. I grinned and let out a breathy laugh; my eyes watered, and I spared one glance at the night sky. *Don't mess this up, Zach!* Meeting his gaze again, I felt my throat close up.

"I didn't want you to see it coming." His eyes sparked with amusement, and I saw a lot more too. A hint of nerves, a whole lot of affection.

"I didn't," I croaked. Way to be cool.

He grabbed my hand in both of his and kissed the top. "I've proposed to you a hundred ways in my head, darling. When you sit on the counter at home and talk about your day while I make dinner. When we get into fights about who misplaced the phone chargers. In bed, in restaurants, during flights." He retrieved his wallet from the inside of his suit pocket, and I exhaled shakily and blinked past the burn. "I even thought about asking you to marry me at the grocery store when you— and I don't know if you've noticed this, but you put my preferred items in the cart first. My Weetabix before your Cap'n Crunch."

"They're so gross," I whispered.

He laughed softly, the warm sound sending a shiver through me. "Ironically, ten minutes later, you dropped the not-so-subtle hint that you preferred white gold over yellow. Which I already knew, by the way." He took my hand again, and my palm brushed against metal. "So I told myself that I was going to make a plan to be spontaneous. I didn't want you to know when. I didn't want you to search through the house for hidden engagement rings."

"It's like you know me."

"A little bit." He held up the ring in his free hand, a simple white-gold band. "I want to keep getting to know you for the rest of my life—as my partner, father to our children, and best friend. Will you be my husband, Zachary?"

I nodded jerkily, about to weep like a fucking baby. "Yeah. Yes. Fuck yes." I wasn't the only one who trembled as he slid the ring onto my finger, thank God. Once it was firmly in place, he surged up and swept me into a deep kiss, and I locked my arms around his neck. "I love you so fucking much, Henry."

He shuddered and kissed me again, nodding slightly. "You're the light of my life," he whispered. "The streak of glitter, even."

I sniffled through a laugh and pressed my forehead to his.

I guess he wasn't done yet. He opened his hand between us, revealing another ring, and the evening went from perfect to…I couldn't even describe it. I took the ring from him and put it where it belonged, then clasped our fingers together.

"Dibs on buying the wedding bands," I said quickly. I had to get that out there. With Henry, you never knew. There was another thing I had to mention as well. "Am I really your best friend?"

"Absolutely, darling. Martin's my oldest."

I smirked. "Don't let him hear the O-word."

"Do you think I'm suicidal?"

I smiled at him, and he smiled back, and it was cheesy as fuck, and I'd gotten the best proposal I could've dreamed of.

I woke up the morning after to the best fucking view. With Henry behind me and his arm outstretched underneath me, our fingers were locked, and I could see the rings glinting in the morning sun. I carefully shifted away from Henry and snatched up my phone from the nightstand, then adjusted our handhold so the rings were more visible before I took a photo of it. I was having this shit framed in every room of the house. Hous*es*.

Henry's sleepy voice startled me. "Let me see."

I turned around in his arms and showed him the photo.

He smiled drowsily. "Perfect."

"Do you mind if I announce it?" I asked. "I could post it to Insta."

"No, go ahead." He nuzzled my neck and pressed a kiss there. "I want the world to know you're my fiancé."

Fiancé. I loved the sound of that.

I posted the photo with only minimal filtering, captioning it, "As of last night, engaged to the man of my dreams. December 9, the day I said yes. And fuck yes."

"There. The world knows." I returned the phone to my night-stand so I could enjoy a morning in bed with my fiancé.

"I think this makes you an official Angelino," he mused.

"Because we're getting married?"

"No, because when New Yorkers place an announcement in the *New York Times,* we in LA use Instagram."

I laughed and nipped at his scruffy chin. "That has to mean I'm more official than you, 'cause you don't have an account—" I was rudely interrupted by the ringing of a phone, and it wasn't even my phone. It was Henry's. "Why are you getting the calls?"

"If it's related," he pointed out and reached for his cell. "And you answered your own question. I'm not on Instagram, so they have to get in touch with me the old-fashioned way. Like normal people—fuck." He grimaced. "It's Joseph."

"Someone's forgotten to unfollow me," I said with a grin.

He sighed and answered the call. "I'm not sure we have anything to say to each other, Joseph." He listened to whatever the asshole had to say, and the more Joseph spoke, the grimmer Henry's expression became. "Are you quite finished? Because I am. I'll miss the friend you used to be, but frankly, I'm beyond ready to get rid of the vindictive person you've become. Zachary's told me everything." I studied Henry's face while Joseph replied, and I could hear him getting heated. So was Henry. "You're damn right that I trust him. For chrissakes, you're living in another universe if you ever believed I—what?" He blew out a breath, frustrated. "The way I see it, I'm not throwing away a fucking thing."

Joseph had more to say, but Henry was done. I could tell.

"Let me say it, *please*," I whispered urgently. "I can't take it anymore."

A spark of rueful amusement lit in Henry's eyes, and he finally —fucking finally—conceded. With a small nod, he let me take over, and I grabbed the phone from him.

Sheer giddiness exploded inside me as I said my piece. "Bye, Felicia!" I ended the call, groaned loudly in relief, and flopped onto my back. "Oh God, was that as good for you as it was for me?"

CHAPTER 8

I STILL WANT MY SWORD FIGHT

"*W*e need to decide on Christmas presents for the boys," Henry said, taking a sip of his coffee. "Sunny-side up for me, please."

I bobbed my head to the beat of the Christmas song playing in the background and flipped my eggs. "Maybe we don't discuss it when they're upstairs?" It was nine o'clock, and they'd be up any moment. The toilet flushed a while ago.

"I probably shouldn't tell you what Martin wants to give them."

Uh, no. Plating the eggs, bacon, and two bagels, I brought the food to the kitchen island and sat down on the stool next to Henry. "Is it a three-letter word?"

"Possibly."

Then, fuck no. It irritated me something fierce. "He's not giving them new cars *again*," I hissed.

"To be fair, it's about upgrading the lease—I see your point." He switched gears at my glare. I drew the line at upgrading vehicles as if they were cell phones. It was fucking insane. Bad enough that they had cars in both Camassia and here. "You'll give Martin the news, yes?"

"*No* problem." I dug my phone out of the pocket of my sweats and sent him a text. The queen could try to guilt me all he wanted; I'd heard it before.

"*I have no kids of my own. What's so wrong with spoiling my pseudo-nephews?*"

Nope, it wouldn't work on me anymore. "I think we should make it a rule that all gifts gotta be able to fit under the tree at home."

"Works for me." He used utensils to eat his bacon. The man was strange. "Is there anything in particular you want?"

"What any gay man wants." I scratched my exposed chest and bit into the crispy bacon. "No soft packages."

Henry chuckled into his coffee mug. "I'll see what I can do."

Let's be honest, though. The best part about Christmas, aside from the food, was the stocking stuffers. Few things topped gift cards and humorous trinkets. Last year, Henry gave me glow-in-the-dark condoms for shits and giggles, but he drew the line at being my Darth Gayder and engaging in a lightsaber fight. No matter how much I begged, he wouldn't go there.

"Penny for your thoughts?" he wondered.

"Lightsabers."

"Oh Jesus Christ, not this again."

I laughed and took a gulp of my juice.

Moments later, a heavy thudding traveled down the stairs, and we looked up to see Ty and Mattie joining us. They were acing the messy bed heads and, like me, wore only sweats. And what in the actual fuck.

"Mattie, when did you pierce your nipple?" I stared at him incredulously.

He yawned and went for the coffeemaker. "I don't know, few months ago. Didn't you see the memo in *Nipples Weekly?*"

Henry snorted. "You're two smartasses in a pod." He eyed Mattie pensively. "Don't let it get infected, though. I've read some horror stories about piercings."

"Yeah, Mattie." Ty slapped my brother's shoulder. "*Horror* stories. Promise Daddy H you'll rub aloe on it every day."

"I'll be careful." Mattie smirked sleepily and sat down with his coffee. Next, a thought hit him because he furrowed his brow at Ty. "I thought we were changing it to Big Poppa."

Or you can just go with Dad...

They made me grin. As we'd slowly morphed into a family, Henry and I had been assigned very different roles. And they thought they were sly when they joked about Henry being the father in the house, but I saw through them. They'd both found something they'd needed in Henry, and it was mutual.

I'd been given the role of older brother, even by Ty, though they respected me a bit more than a regular brother. They asked me for permission and stuff when they knew it was necessary, but it was Henry who received papers from school and whenever they needed something signed.

Henry ate that shit up.

Breakfast continued amidst mindless chatter and more food being added to the island. Henry and Mattie took turns with the various sections of the paper, Ty was scribbling notes on his digital sketchpad, and I scrolled through my notifications on Instagram. Given the number of complete strangers that followed me now, I had to sift through a lot of heart-eyes emojis before I found comments from actual friends.

Which reminded me... "By the way, we're engaged," I told the guys.

Their heads snapped up, a dual, "What?" slipping out.

"I asked Zachary to marry me last night." Henry kissed my temple.

"That's awesome. Congrats, guys," Ty said with a smile.

"Yeah, congratulations." Mattie nodded and refolded his paper. "Maybe Zach can stop filling his Pinterest boards with engagement ideas now."

I had no idea what he was talking about. Ty and Henry clearly did, 'cause they thought it was worth some serious laughing at.

"I don't know how Pinterest works," I defended. "I'm not even on there!"

"That's so funny," Henry chuckled and pulled out his phone. "I have to tell Martin."

I rolled my eyes.

❈

"You're such a couch hog, darling."

"I know, this is *amazing*." I stretched out further and bit his flannel-covered thigh playfully. He was the best pillow in the world, and this was a seriously fantastic couch. The L-shaped slice of heaven divided the living room and kitchen, meaning the cupboards of snacks were never far away. The coffee table was full already, and we had the latest season of *The Walking Dead* playing to complete the perfect engagement celebration.

Henry combed my hair back with his fingers and smiled down at me. "You're happy."

"I'm fucking blissful." I'd be even happier if he lost his tee. I liked having a masculine chest to ogle. "What about you?"

He stroked my cheek. "If the old me met me today, I would've found this new version obnoxious for how happy he is." He nodded at the table. "Hand me some of those gummy bears, will you?"

Ah, my snob. Regular ones weren't good enough. He bought this stuff at some upscale boutique in Beverly Hills and kept it hidden from Mattie and Ty. I wasn't going to admit I loved the candy too. I had a reputation to uphold.

He took the colorful pieces and tossed a couple into his mouth. "When do you want us to speak to Mattie?"

I checked the clock above the flat screen. "Before I step out to get us dinner—or whenever he has the time." I looked back up at Henry. "Is Ty going up to Malibu tonight?"

He nodded, and I wasn't surprised. Ty usually spent the night above the bookstore and had dinner with Martin when he didn't have classes the day after. As for Mattie, he was trickier to pin down. He was upstairs studying right now, and he had class later. There was something about a study group too. He had too much going on.

Henry and I spent the next few hours cuddling our asses off, eating too many snacks, drinking sodas until we almost burst, and losing a few characters on *The Walking Dead*. Mattie came down here and there, only to get a drink before running up again.

In between episodes, I responded to messages from friends congratulating us on the engagement, and Henry had a minor bitch fight with Martin about everything from the wedding, engagement party, to the boys' Christmas gifts.

"Just let him host a damn party," I said, biting off a piece of candy. Coke-flavored gummy worms this time. I'd already finished the chocolate and probably gained a ton. Brooklyn was gonna love that.

"He wants us to extend our stay," Henry replied. "That's why I said no."

"Oh. Good boy."

He cocked a brow at me. "Careful, Zachary."

I poked his nose. "Boop."

His eyes lit up with laughter, though he actually managed to keep from grinning.

"You two are nauseatingly sweet." Mattie was at the bottom of the stairs, and he pretended to gag before veering right for the kitchen. "What's for dinner?"

"Benny's Tacos." I sat up and ran a hand through my hair. "You look tired, little brother."

He lifted a shoulder and grabbed a bottle of water. "I gotta hand in a paper tomorrow."

Henry cleared his throat and sat forward a bit. "Sit with us for a moment, Mattie. Zachary and I have some concerns we'd like to discuss with you."

Mattie wasn't used to being in trouble, so he always got this wary look on his face when someone wanted to talk. Closing the fridge, he walked over and sat down on the short end of the couch.

"What's up?" He reached for a bag of chips but didn't open it.

"We think you've signed up for too many classes," I stated.

He frowned. "The more classes I take now, the easier it'll be when I've picked my major next year." He'd long since zeroed in on engineering, and I'd been told they often went into their field earlier.

Henry leaned forward and rested his elbows on his knees. "There's no rush, though, sweetheart. If this is about your scholarship—"

"Fuck the fucking scholarship," I said. "Mattie, I'm finally in a position where I can pay for your education. But you insist on this shit, and it's turning you into a zombie. When was the last time you slept eight hours?"

"That's not a thing," Mattie joked. "People don't actually sleep that long."

I stared at him, not finding it funny. Dammit, he was too much like me. Even now, thinking back on what I said just ten seconds ago... Henry had been offering to help Mattie for as long as we'd known him. Mattie refused. My brother had been busting his ass to get perfect scores for years, and I wasn't sure he knew how to power down and take it easy. Kinda like I'd struggled— and still did. Henry and I could go fifty-fifty on everyday stuff, and the fact that it was my name on the mortgage here in Santa Monica provided a fuzzy blanket of comfort. But it was bullshit.

"Fuck this." I gripped my hair, realizing what I had to do. It was time to accept and go all in. At that thought, I glanced at my hand. At my ring. *All in.* "Okay." I swallowed. "From now on, we'll do the merge thing." I waved a hand, uncomfortable as fuck. "It's not about Henry paying for your college or me paying. It's us. You're working yourself into an early grave because you put yourself on a deadline and think you're gonna lose the scholarship."

Henry shifted closer and threaded our fingers together, holding my hand firmly.

"But I'm fine, guys," Mattie insisted. "I have...maybe ten more days of this. I'll hand in my paper and finish the damn Calculus that's hanging over my head, and then I'll have two weeks off. Plenty of time to rest, right?"

Yeah, and then what?

Mattie rose from the couch and smirked tiredly. "I'm serious. I appreciate what you're doing, but I'm fine."

I didn't believe him. I knew my brother's tells, and he was more anxious lately. I'd missed it somehow, which made me feel horrible.

Mattie returned upstairs.

I tilted my head at Henry.

"We'll convince him when he comes home for Christmas," he murmured.

I nodded.

"Did you mean it?" he wondered.

I knew he was talking about the finances, and I nodded again. "I'm sorry it took me a while."

He shook his head and pressed his lips to my forehead. "You and Dominic are the same."

What? The mention of my buddy from back home caught me off guard at first. Then I realized Henry was right. Given Dominic's rough past, one where money mattered the most because nothing else would keep you fed for the day, he'd struggled a lot to accept what Adrian did for him. Their circumstance was more extreme than ours, yet the principle was the same.

Henry kept reminding me that much of his wealth was inherited; there was our age difference, and there were things more important than money in our situation. It was about time I listened to him.

Shrugging on my leather jacket, I walked over to the kitchen island and wrote a note for the boys while Henry took our luggage out to the cab.

Good morning, Earthlings

We expect you at home on the twentieth. Martin will be here with dinner on Wednesday, don't forget. Call us if you need anything.
Love you both,

Zach & Henry

"Are you ready?" Henry asked.

I nodded and left the kitchen. "I found a receipt for the cleaning service, so I used your credit card to pay for the next month." It would give Mattie—and Ty—less to worry about.

"Our credit card, you mean?" He smirked faintly.

"Baby steps, man. I used it. Focus on that."

He chuckled and ushered me outside. Then we took the Uber to LAX and managed to beat traffic—or traffic by LA standards. Breakfast in the lounge led to celebratory mimosas because we were finally going home.

The flight was uneventful, as was the ride up to Camassia, and I couldn't fucking stop smiling. Washington was covered in snow, and after just recovering from a three-day blizzard, there were reports of a storm much worse rolling in. Thank you, Canada!

Neither Henry nor I wanted to leave the house for a while once we got home, so as soon as we entered the town limits, we visited Nan and then went grocery shopping.

"I'm gonna be naked the entire time," I declared.

"It's the holiday season, darling. I want candles lit everywhere to make it truly cozy."

"Okay, so I'll wear fireproof boxers."

"And definitely no sword fights."

I looked to him accusingly. "Funsucker."

He laughed. "Cocksucker."

Hnngh.

Nothing could ruin my Christmas now.

CHAPTER 9

FORGIVE ME, FATHER, FOR I HATE SEXATHONS

Day four of being home alone with my fiancé, two dogs, and one cat:
I'm loving life.

"Something smells awesome, baby," I said absently, scrolling down on my laptop. We'd officially welcomed the snowstorm of the century, and that meant online shopping. While I occupied the sofa in the living room, Henry was experimenting with making holiday candy.

"I think this batch will be successful." He was trying a recipe for fudge that Martin had sent him. "Would you like some more hot cocoa? I'll bring it to you."

I grinned to myself, finding him too fucking cute. He was in his Christmassy doting mood, and I got everything handed to me. In his words, it had to be perfect. Soft Christmas music was playing in the background, the tree glowed red, green, and gold with its lights and decorations, the dogs were napping on the rug in front of the fire, and there was always a delicious smell coming from the kitchen. When he'd told me he was obsessed with the holidays, he hadn't been lying.

To top it all off, the snow was coming down hard outside the big floor-to-ceiling windows. The river was just a blanket of white.

"Do you think Martin will like bunny slippers as a stocking stuffer?" I asked.

"Describe them for me." He wrestled with a bag of mini marshmallows as I caught his reflection in the window.

"They're pink, and one says 'Fucking,' and the other says 'Like.' There're sparkles on the bunny ears too."

Henry laughed. "You have to get them."

That's what I was thinking. We had six stockings hanging over the fireplace, and I wanted them all full of funny shit.

Since my laptop and phone were synced, the alert for a text from Martin popped up in the middle of my shopping spree.

I have to tell someone, but you cannot tell Henry. I saw my ex last night, and it was amazing. Picture me drawing out the word. That amazing! Don't tell Henry.

"Henry! Martin's with the car thief again, and I can't tell you."

"I *swear*," Henry growled. "What the hell is wrong with him? You know what, I won't help him this time. When his car gets stolen, I'll give him the number to a car dealer. Mark my words."

I wasn't gonna mark them.

He came over with a mug of steaming hot chocolate, topped with whipped cream and marshmallows. "Ask him what happened to that nice man he was dating before Thanksgiving."

I complied, firing off a reply.

What happened to Thomas?

"Thank you." I accepted the mug and took a slow sip, then licked the excess cream off my upper lip, and Henry sank down on the couch next to me. "He's typing."

He turned forty.

"We shouldn't have asked." I shook my head.

Henry sighed. "He does like those twenty-five-year-olds."

The following day, I found myself pacing restlessly in front of the coffee table while Henry was out running errands. I checked the time every twenty seconds, and the TV was showing the local weather. It was horrid out there, yet he'd insisted. Okay, we couldn't very well let the dogs go without food, but the *other* errand...

I wanted it, I didn't want it, I was curious, I was a little freaked out.

This was what happened when you were tipsy on Christmas cocktails. You had the most bizarre ideas. I bit my thumbnail anxiously, before I finally saw the headlights of Henry's Jeep piercing through the heavy snowfall.

I sent off a quick text to Dominic.

Okay, he's back.

He was as fast with his response.

Lemme know if Adrian and I should try it.

I tossed the phone on the couch as the garage doors closed below us, and I waited by the door until I heard him walk up the stairs. Then I ripped the door open and hauled him inside.

"Did it work?" I helped him shed his coat, and I flinched at the snowflakes that rolled off his shoulders. "Did you get it?"

"I got it," he chuckled.

"This is crazy, right?" I followed him into the kitchen where he stowed away the kibble.

"Well, I wasn't planning on trying them for another ten years, but..."

But, yeah. We were gonna try Viagra together.

"I fear I wasn't convincing enough," he added. "The doctor would only prescribe me a few single-packets." He retrieved three little packets and placed them on the counter.

I leaned over them and stared as if they were going to put on a show.

I could blame Henry for this. He'd spiked the drinks, and then we'd somehow started talking about porn, and I mentioned having read that porn stars took extra stimulants sometimes. And I was a curious guy, okay?

"Let's do it," I said.

Ten minutes later, we were seated on the couch with glasses of water and each holding up a little blue pill, eyeing them suspiciously.

"How long do they last?" I asked.

"Up to five hours." He pinched the pill between his fingers and sniffed at it. "It's likely it'll last longer for me because your metabolism is faster."

"Interesting. Should I get the fly swatter to ward off your advances when I'm over it?"

A corner of his mouth twisted up. "We've established your safeword by now."

I nodded. "Safeword, safeword, my fiancé's priapism is trying to fuck me, safeword!"

"You have to say that exact sentence. In that order. Otherwise, I won't stop."

I chuckled, eyeing the pill one more time. *Here we go. Fuck like there's no tomorrow.* I chased down the pill with two gulps of water, and Henry followed suit.

Now we wait.

I drummed my fingers along my leg. "When will we know?"

"The doctor said it usually works after about half an hour, but never without some sort of stimulation."

Leaning back against the cushions, I crooked a finger at him. "C'mere, my beast. Let me stimulate you."

I loved sex.

I admit, the first round on the couch was over embarrassingly quickly, but the recovery time was fucking amazing. We just had to think sexy thoughts and make out for the arousal to come roaring back.

"How do you want me?" I walked backward to our bed and pushed down my sweats.

He unzipped his jeans and watched me as I got on the bed. "Socks too, dear. We're not animals."

"You didn't have a problem with them when you bent me over the couch ten minutes ago."

"That's entirely different, and I didn't have your feet in my face. Off with them, now."

"Yes, Daddy." I rolled my eyes and slipped off my supercomfy wool socks. "Forgive my sock sins."

His mouth twitched. "You're mixing two kinks there."

I bit my lip as the images of confessing my filthy sins to Henry flooded my mind, and I rose to my knees on the bed. My cock continued to throb, and Henry stepped closer and gently wrapped his fingers around me.

I looked down, staring at the way he stroked me. Ghosting touches, frustratingly so.

"Fuck me," I breathed. I thrust into his hold. The blood surged, and it was bordering on uncomfortable. "Please? I need it."

He hummed and joined me on the bed, getting comfortable on his back, and he reached for the lube. "Come here and sit on my cock."

The heat exploded within, and I cursed.

He wanted me with my back to him, so I hiked a leg over his upper body and straddled his thighs. Next, he asked if I could reach the remote at the foot of the bed.

"I had to watch something while you were in LA," he murmured.

I pushed play on the DVD while he slicked up his cock. No use in fingering me first. I was already wet and ready from our last round, and I hoped this wouldn't be over as quickly. The flat screen lit up with the last time we filmed ourselves fucking.

"Sink down on me," he commanded huskily.

With my hands planted on his knees, I inched back until the head of his cock rubbed against my ass. Raising myself up slightly, I angled us better and then took him inside inch by inch. I moaned under my breath and gripped my dick tightly. He filled me so perfectly, stretching my ass to the max.

"Goddamn, I love your cock," I blurted breathlessly. "I feel so full." I eased forward, then backward harder. "*Ungh.* If you were my priest, I'd tell you anything."

He grunted then sucked in a breath, his hands coming to my hips. "We can always pretend. Go on and confess your sins to your Father."

"Oh God," I mumbled. My face flushed, and I caught a glance at the TV where Henry was fucking me roughly into the mattress. "I think...I think about being taken against my will, F-Father. I fantasize about you—fucking me at night, shushing me, saying you can't get enough of your baby boy's little ass."

"Go on, son," he whispered raggedly.

Fueled by my fantasies and the unmistakable lust in his voice, I fucked myself on Henry's cock harder and faster.

"You keep a hand over my mouth because it's a secret." I bit out a groan and took him all the way in, and I rolled my hips.

He gripped my hips tighter and pushed into me. "Will you be begging me to stop?"

I nodded and swallowed dryly. It was the fantasy of him shushing me that drove me crazy. "*Shh, just take me, son.*" I'd pretend to fight him, and he would groan lustfully in my ear and fondle my cock. "*I can't help myself when you parade that sweet little ass around. I have to take it, make it mine, fill it with my come until you can't take another drop.*"

I was too horny and needy to care about my embarrassment,

so I managed to get the thoughts out in between groans, gasps, and thrusts.

Henry's reaction to my confession was to push me onto all fours and shove his cock so hard inside me that all the air in my lungs left me in a whoosh. Standing on one leg and with one foot planted on the mattress, his fingers digging painfully into my hips, he fucked me so he brushed against my prostate on most passes.

"*Fuck!*"

"Push back on me, baby boy," he ordered. "I need you to push back."

The pain and pleasure zinged through me, creating a whirlwind of urgency. I pushed back on every painful thrust, my body's aches irrelevant. My brain was screaming at me to get more, more, more, and the arousal kept assaulting me.

Henry groaned. "Harder."

That word, along with "faster," became the theme. I lost count of the positions we tried, how long we were at it, and it was impossible to measure how desperately we needed to get off.

At one point, I almost started crying. The bliss mingled with aggravation, because I couldn't. Fucking. Get. There.

I stroked myself quickly and shut my eyes. The sound of skin slapping increased as we struggled to sate our needs. My orgasm finally started approaching, but it felt different. I didn't know how or why.

"*Henry,*" I gritted out. Strung tight and flushed all over, I did everything I could to make it go faster. "Make me come." I whimpered in between gasps. "Oh God, I gotta come."

He growled a curse and pulled out. "Get on your back," he snapped. "Fuck." He blew out a breath as I scrambled into position, and he looked as frustrated as I felt. "If we die today, I want my headstone to make it clear it was your fault, you cock-hungry little slut."

"I accept that." I spread my legs for him and pulled him down for a hard, messy kiss. At the same time, he rammed his cock inside me, and I winced and cried out hoarsely at the pain. Yet…it pushed me closer to my climax. A long moan escaped me, and I began jacking my dick again. "Fuck me—just take me," I pleaded. "I'm almost there."

"Me too." He pounded in and out of me and grabbed my throat in a light chokehold. "Oh hell, darling."

"How strong are those motherfucking pills?" I panted.

"Hundred milligrams."

"A hundred—!" My eyes flew open wide. I didn't know squat about dosage, but it sounded like a lot!

"Shh, the slut talks too much."

He shushed me.

The fire spread in my veins, and the orgasm crashed down on me without warning. Clenching around him as tightly as I could, I took all the cock he gave me and felt ropes of come landing on my stomach and chest. But it was wrong, it was fucking wrong, it was so wrong. The desire didn't lessen as it normally would.

Henry bit out another growl and started coming too.

Meanwhile, I let out a choked cry 'cause I had to have more.

Think unsexy thoughts, think unsexy thoughts. I wasn't gonna lose my erection unless I quit thinking about him tearing into me. Filling me. Marking me. Kissing me.

"Motherfucking…what the…" Henry was panting and peering down between us, and I instinctively shifted my hips to bring him deeper. "You're joking with this. I can't—Jesus Christ."

"More," I complained. *"Move."*

He shuddered and shot me a heated glare. "You'll be the death of me, Zachary."

"You need more too, don't you?"

He swallowed and nodded once, then pulled out. "Get in the shower. I have an idea."

Dragging my exhausted self off the bed and into the bathroom, I flinched and stroked my chafing cock. Lustful thoughts, like rubbing come into my skin, were as effective as fighting a fire with gasoline. Hell, even my arm was sore. Could I even jerk myself with my left? I wasn't a superhero, man. Or, you know, left-handed.

The feeling of Henry's release seeping out of my asshole didn't exactly stop the blood flow to my cock.

I turned the water on cold and hissed, stepping under the spray. One forearm landed on the tiles, and I rested my forehead there. Another hiss slipped through clenched teeth because the chilled water sluiced between my ass cheeks and across my hypersensitive skin. Unfortunately, it felt amazing too. The cold water drops tickled and caressed, and I groaned and rolled my eyes at my own whorishness. Great. I was getting turned on by water.

Henry appeared in the door, and he was ripping into some kind of packaging. "I was going to give you this for Christmas." It looked like a travel mug or one of those plastic tumblers, except... *Oh.*

"Is that a Fleshjack?" Yeah, there was no way I'd kill my hard-on. "I love you so much right now."

Henry smiled faintly and joined me in the shower. "It has a shower mount." He handed me the fuck device, the crystal-clear tumbler with a silicone butthole, and I stuck a finger into the hole. Oh, that was gonna feel so damn good.

"I'm naming it Captain Ass Tumbler," I declared. While Henry fastened the suction cup to the wall, I tested the toy, pushing my dick inside. "Jesus, I'm never using my hand again." It was tight, ribbed for my pleasure, and seriously fantastic. "Hello, my second favorite lover."

"Here we go." Henry robbed me of the pleasure when he took the Fleshjack from me, though only to attach it to the shower mount. "I fuck you, you fuck this." The authority in his voice drew me in like nothing else.

"Yes, Daddy." I stole a kiss to silence his chuckle before he got behind me, and I planted my hands on the wall. My cock nudged the silicone, and I inched forward slowly to let the shivers run through me. "Holy fuck. I need your cock."

"I'm going to film this one day. We could add some role-play..." He pressed a kiss to my shoulder, licking off the water beating down on us, and guided his thick cock to my ass. "Does Daddy's little baby need more lube?"

I moaned at his dirty talk like the whore I was.

"Fair enough." He caught me off guard when he rammed into me, and it sent me flying forward, effectively burying my cock in the mounted toy. "The sounds you make, darling boy."

I whimpered. The plastic sleeve of the toy was clear and see-through, so I could see my cock penetrating the tight silicone. Combined with Henry taking my ass, it made me spiral out of control.

The fuckfest continued.

"No, you stay over there!" I let out a pitiful moan and buried my face in the couch cushion. "Henry, I'm dying."

"I have to rub some aloe—"

"No," I grated. "Don't you get it? I'll get hard again, and then I'll die."

We were on the fourth hour. Supposedly, Viagra stopped working after five. I'd be the judge of that. Either way, four hours of fucking was completely insane, and I wasn't having sex again, ever—for a few days.

Henry sighed impatiently and gently pulled down my pajama bottoms. "You're red, sweetheart. Let me make you feel better."

"Bastard," I whispered into the cushion. "I want to kick you in the jingle balls for this."

He chuckled warmly, and then I had cold lotion rubbed into

my ass. Thank fuck my dick didn't respond with more than a few lazy twitches.

"Need I remind you this was your idea?" he asked. "Thanks to you, I can barely walk, and my doctor thinks I have erectile dysfunction."

"You said he probably didn't believe you," I grumbled. We were so flushing the third single-pack we'd gotten. "Mmm, keep going."

He was fingering me lightly with an aloe-coated pinkie.

I was a fan.

Henry snorted and withdrew his finger, then readjusted my PJ bottoms. "Slut. Let me make you dinner instead."

"Bangers and mash seem very appropriate," I noted.

"I was thinking rump roast, actually."

I giggled like a girl. "Don't forget to wash your hands!"

By the time the kitchen and living room smelled like food again, I was ready to try sitting up. I winced and bitched but managed to find an angle that didn't feel like being fucked by a knife.

"God..." My head lolled back, and little Lady jumped up on the couch for a snuggle. "Yeah, comfort Daddy."

Henry came over to serve me a glass of Coke, crushed cherries, and ice. Because he was the best. "There's a splash of rum in there."

"Yum." I leaned forward with a grunt and took a sip. "Perfect —" My phone buzzed on the table. "Can't. Reach."

"My poor cripple." He looked at me in amusement and handed me my phone. "Dinner should be ready in twenty."

"I don't deserve you," I sighed contentedly.

Lady licked my cheek.

Then I frowned as I read the text from Ty.

I don't want to alarm you guys, but Mattie just dropped out of college and went on tour with a rock band. That's all.

CHAPTER 10

PHILADELPHIA IS NOT IN WASHINGTON

"*Y*ou really couldn't find *anything?*" I paced the living room floor, listening to Martin prattling on about everyone he'd called in order to find out who Mattie was running off with.

Henry was on the phone too.

"Ty is calling the numbers he has," Martin replied. "So far, we only have the city."

I looked over to Henry as he covered the mouthpiece on his phone. "We can get on the red-eye if we leave now. Should I book the tickets?"

Ugh. I clenched my jaw, then sighed heavily. Hadn't Mexico been enough? Now we were going all across the country to track down my brother who *stupidly* wouldn't answer the phone.

"Yeah, might as well." I slumped down on the couch and gripped my hair, ignoring the pain in my ass. "Okay, we're booking flights. Can you keep asking around, Martin?"

"Try to stop me," he retorted. "My boy's alone out there in the wild, Zach."

I grinned faintly and drummed my fingers along my mouth. "Has anyone ever called you a drama queen?"

"Not that I recall," he answered thoughtfully. "Bring Mattie home, you hear? I'll call you if I find out anything new."

"Okay. Later, hon." I ended the call and looked up at Henry. "Remember when we said we weren't gonna leave Washington in December? That was funny."

Henry smiled ruefully. "Too good to be true, that's what it was. Let's go pack. We have to leave in ten minutes."

I followed him up the stairs, reluctant as fuck, and once in the bedroom, I hauled out our rollaboard luggage while he called the pet sitter. She was gonna get a raise, I reckoned. We didn't even know exactly when we'd be home again.

"This is so unlike my brother," I muttered to myself. Entering our closet, I grabbed tees, a couple button-downs, jeans, and slacks for us. Henry had underwear, socks, and toiletries covered. "Seriously, dropped *out*? Completely?"

Ty's initial text had obviously made him the recipient of all our questions, but he didn't know much. He could tell us that Mattie had started hanging out with musicians a while back, and apparently, my brother took an interest in the drums. I remembered him mentioning it before Mexico, though none of that explained why he'd up and leave everything to go on a tour. People didn't just *do* that. Additionally, you didn't pick up an instrument and master it in a few months.

"Breaking points push us to extremes sometimes." Henry's comment made me uneasy, because he'd voiced what I feared. It was the reason we were flying to Philadelphia rather than waiting and hoping for the best.

Philadelphia. An outdoor concert tomorrow—in the dead of winter. Google had helped us pinpoint the exact time and place, and that was all we had to go on. Oh, and Dominic—who'd lived there once—had told us how to get to the concert venue.

Martin was in the process of looking up all the bands attending to see which ones were based in California.

Whereas I dressed for comfort in sweats and a matching

hoodie, Henry donned an Armani suit. "Travel sharp and well," he liked to say.

My snob wasn't gonna sleep as well as I did on the plane.

We made it to Sea-Tac in record time, despite the weather that delayed our flight. It was almost midnight when we boarded, and Martin had texted us a final clue.

One of the bands attending the outdoor concert was not only based in Los Angeles, but the singer was from "northern Washington." For all I knew, they could've met at home.

"Could it be from high school?" I asked, buckling my seat belt. A flight attendant came over and asked if we wanted something to drink while they boarded coach, but what I wanted—like, fucking clarity—wasn't on the menu.

"I have no idea," Henry murmured as he scrolled through his phone. "It would be so much easier if I had a name to go on."

"Oh," I said. "Sorry, I thought I mentioned it. Jesse Novak is the singer, according to Martin."

"Novak." Henry looked straight ahead and knitted his brows together. "Where have I heard that before?"

No clue. It would be awesome if he remembered.

Hopefully, I could sleep all the way to Philadelphia. We'd done everything we could. We'd bought tickets to this concert, we'd messaged Mattie on every social media platform he was on, and we'd booked a hotel room and confirmed an early check-in. Martin was also going to try to contact the organizers behind the event. Maybe they could help us somehow.

As the plane taxied out, Henry pocketed his phone and loosened his tie. Once we were in the air, he was gonna go through his red-eye routine of setting aside his shoes, removing his tie, hanging up his suit jacket, and picking some foreign film to fall asleep to. He had a similar morning routine, except it included taking his toiletry bag to the bathroom instead of picking a movie.

"I wanna be cute with you," I said. "Hold my hand?"

He chuckled a little and linked our fingers together on the armrests between us.

"We are so far away from Camassia…" I yawned, pulled the hood of my sweater over my head, and zipped up my ski jacket as far as it went. Philly greeted us frigidly, and the line for the cabs was ridiculously long.

Henry, who was still growing reaccustomed to colder climates after spending so many years in LA, rocked his wool overcoat. He was the picture of a sexy businessman, leather gloves included. Though, he was only wearing one at the moment because he wouldn't let go of his phone. He was driving himself crazy with the last name he couldn't place but was sure he'd heard before.

"Almost our turn, honey." I nudged our bags closer to the front of the line with my foot.

I'd never been to Philly before.

Moments later, we got in a cab and headed toward downtown where our hotel was. The skyline looked cool, and there was a trickle of excitement to see a new city.

"Aha, I knew it," Henry said. "I was searching in the wrong place, but I was certain I'd heard Novak before. Abel Hayes, remember him?"

I nodded. He was the son of a couple Henry worked with back home. The wife, Adeline, ran a facility and safe place where victims of abuse could recover and get back on their feet. Henry hadn't thought twice about getting involved in the organization. Lincoln, Adeline's husband, was a music producer. He was probably best known as the former guitar player of Path of Destruction, an old rock band.

"He's a hockey player, right?" I recalled Abel was into hockey.

"Indeed, he plays for the Canucks. Know what else?" Henry showed me his phone. "His full name is Abel Novak-Hayes."

I frowned, confused. That Abel and his brother were adopted was not news, but...wait. His brother. "Abel's brother—didn't he live in LA?"

Henry inclined his head. "And that's Jesse. Whether Mattie met him at the fundraiser in Seattle last fall, or they somehow ran into each other in LA, I don't know. But this means I'm going to call Adeline the minute they wake up on the West Coast."

That was a relief. She of all people should know how to get in touch with Jesse, and by default, Mattie.

"You're the sexiest Sherlock that ever Sherlocked," I said.

He smirked. "Would you like to be my Watson?"

"As long as Watson gets fucked, because I'm doing my Kegels right now."

Clench.

Henry was on the phone while I showered off the plane ride and a too-brief nap, and when I came out with a towel wrapped around my hips, he was just wrapping up the call.

"Of course, I'll let you know. And apologies again for calling so early." He placed the phone between his cheek and shoulder so he could hang up his shirts in the closet. People actually did that —used the hotel closet for clothes. "You too, Adeline. Give Nova-Lyn my best." He smiled, referring to Adeline and Lincoln's daughter. "Will do. Bye now."

"How did it go?" I asked.

He'd already unpacked my stuff, which otherwise stayed in the suitcase, 'cause why not? So I dug out a pair of tight briefs that Henry got his rocks off seeing me in. I was more of a boxer briefs guy when it came to Henry and what I liked seeing him in. But he had those fantastic thighs. When the fabric stretched around his muscles, I went into gawk mode.

"Adeline spoke to Jesse," he replied and walked closer. "Mattie has asked not to talk to anyone, so Jesse was torn." I put my hands on my hips while Henry "adjusted" my cock. It was one of his things. To make sure it was *just so*. "He wouldn't let us pass along a message, but he put us on the list so we'll have backstage access after the show—actually, let me just..." He sank to one knee, pulled down my briefs, and pressed his face to the sensitive spot where thigh met crotch.

I trembled and let out a long "Hhnghh" sound, my hands falling to his shoulders. "Jesus, Henry. Warnings—what have we said about them?"

"Not a fan." He hummed and licked the length of my dick. "You can't have it both ways, darling boy. Either you want me to catch you off guard, or you want to be warned."

Touché. Forget what I was saying.

"Go on," I rasped.

He made an appreciative sound and sucked me strongly into his mouth, swirling his tongue around me as I thickened and grew harder.

It wasn't like we had any plans before the concert...

At six o'clock, we left the hotel in our warmest clothes and started the trek toward the concert venue. Henry explained he hadn't been in Philadelphia for many years but remembered the location was near the Liberty Bell. Five minutes of walking in snowfall was enough for me to call bullshit on the "within walking distance" claim.

Los Angeles had spoiled me. No one walked there.

Grabbing Henry's glove-covered hand, I inched closer to him as we shared the sidewalk with way too many people. There was an atmosphere about the city I liked, though. The downtown area wasn't huge, and it was less crazy than New York. Despite the cold, I smiled a little and looked up at the darkening sky. The tall buildings here weren't exactly the norm back home, or in what we called the earthquake zone.

You're not in Camassia anymore, Zachary...

"Disgusting fags," someone muttered as he passed.

The anger unfurled instantly, and I turned around to—

"Keep walking, my love." Henry had a tight grip on my arm and moved me forward. I huffed and nearly stumbled. "You're better than that."

"I'll happily prove you wrong," I spat angrily under my breath. "Jesus Christ. How can you let that shit slide?"

I knew I was lucky. We never ran into trouble in LA, and once Pammie took over managing the store, I stopped encountering the worst hicks. I caught a sneer and the rare comment here and there, but it was bearable, though it still angered me.

"Because the odds are in my favor," he told me, "that one day, his niece, child, or friend's kid will look at him and call him an uneducated bigot. They won't respect him, nor think he's macho. The man back there will become entirely irrelevant. Worthless. His opinion will have no meaning whatsoever, and he'll hate it."

"You can't know that," I replied, irritated. "You can't be sure people will change."

"Individually? No. But remember, I speak from experience, Zachary." Henry gave me a wry glance. "This is why we educate and work to raise awareness, so that the next generation will have better opportunities. When I was your age, there were few places I'd hold another man's hand in public. Slurs and insults were the mildest attack back then."

I frowned at the wet ground, processing what he'd said. The

patience Henry possessed...I didn't have a fraction of it. My temper got the best of me when idiots needed to be schooled.

"So it's always for the next generation," I said quietly.

"If we're lucky, we get to see the hard work paying off." He pressed a kiss to my temple. "I see it every day, and it'll get even better. In the meantime, we keep working, and we try to teach people tolerance. Including fools like Martin."

I chuckled once, having witnessed their political fights a few times. Martin called himself fiscally conservative and socially liberal, something that drove Henry mad.

"I think it's time I get involved in Second Family," I admitted. "I should help. I want to. And I'm marrying this hot sugar daddy, so I guess I can afford it."

Henry laughed and hugged me to him. "Look at you, making such progress. Daddy's very proud."

"*Hnngh*, that's so hot."

I quit the jokes, my mind already spinning on this. I could split my time between ShadowLight and Second Family, maybe get some exposure for the nonprofit through the modeling gigs? Brooklyn's husband and brother-in-law's organization for rescue dogs already had a Pet Buddy project with Second Family for LGBTQ+ people who were afraid to be alone.

For some reason, people listened to me. I'd brushed off Brooklyn's talk about YouTube ratings and how my videos were generally the most popular, because I was crap at accepting praise. Perhaps it was time to use it to build my career, a lasting one.

"This could actually become something." I was getting increasingly pumped to get involved, and I explained my thoughts to Henry about spokesperson stuff and what I could do to gain exposure. "And the whole point of her diversity campaign was to raise awareness, so I don't see her flat-out refusing," I went on. "I think I need to talk to her after the holidays."

"And out of the hellfire of hatred, rises the voice of—"

"Oh my God, stop it, Lord Byron."

"You couldn't have chosen a less deviant poet?"

Nah.

"Ticket admission is over there." I pointed across the street.

There was a huge lawn, and a stage was taking up the northern end of it. Music blared out, distorted by the winds, and the spotlights traveled across the audience. Beer tents and merchandise vendors had people crowding this side of the area, and there were plenty of people moving around outside the fences too.

Crossing the street, Henry retrieved our printed tickets from the inside of his coat, and he handed me one.

"Let me know if you see anyone handing out programs," he requested.

I stifled my smirk. "This is a rock concert, baby, not a show on Broadway."

He peered down at me, brows knitted. "No programs?"

I shrugged. "Online, sure, and you'll probably find posters with the lineup."

"Hmph." He muttered something as an "aside" that they were called playbills on Broadway, but I tuned out the adorable nut. "How do collectors save anything from rock shows, then?"

"Apparel." I got a kick out of this. "I think most buy hoodies with the lineup or the tour name on the back."

"A bit difficult to put in an album." He sniffed and handed his ticket over to the girl in the ticket booth. "Good evening."

"Your hand," she said.

"Pardon?" Henry looked confused.

I grinned, gave her my ticket, and stuck out my hand to get it stamped.

"Ah." My man wasn't humored for shit, but he removed a

glove and let her press the bright blue stamp onto his skin. As we entered the concert area, he looked at it in dismay. "It's smeared already."

"I love you," I laughed.

"I'm so glad I amuse you," he drawled. "Now, where can we find Mattie?"

"I guess we wait." I slipped my hand into his and eyed the vendors around us. Jesse's band was one of the last ones to go on, and we'd timed it so we got here halfway through the event. "Let's grab some outrageously expensive shitty beer and hot dogs."

"When you put it like that…"

For the first ten or fifteen minutes, Henry was the epitome of upper class who, though he was always too humble to ever look down on anyone, definitely struggled with the "mess of things." The ground was wet and muddy, the bar tables were sticky, and the sight of port-a-johns made him look so horrified that I guffawed until I couldn't breathe.

This was the man who had no issues with going hunting, fishing, *gutting* fish, and getting his hands dirty.

"That's different," he argued. "There's a time and place, and I don't wear dress shoes in the woods." He grimaced as he stepped in a small puddle of snow and mud.

Okay, time to turn his frown upside down. To my shock, I'd learned he'd never eaten a pretzel before, so that was next on the menu—since he'd made a face and declined the hot dog. Which was fucking delicious if you asked me.

He bitched about not being hungry the entire time we waited in line, then muttered under his breath as I ordered two soft pretzels and paid for them, then sighed heavily as I tore into a packet of mustard and shoved the pretzel in his face.

"Try it," I ordered.

He surrendered with another quiet scoff and dipped the

pretzel in the mustard. Then he took a small bite and chewed it slowly.

I bit into mine with a grin.

Henry was silent for a moment. He swallowed the salted bread and took himself another taste, this one bigger. More mustard.

"My goodness." He brushed salt flakes off his chest and bit into the pretzel properly.

"You like it. You really, really *like* it."

"Don't tell Martin—but God. These are amazing."

That was only the beginning. It was a rock concert, not a county fair, so the options were limited once Henry admitted that he didn't have much experience with festival foods.

"Mother would never let Thorne and me eat street food," he said.

Poor guy. It was my responsibility to change that, so I looked around to see if there were any other edibles, and I came up kinda empty. Unless he wanted to try crappy pizza or candied almonds—actually...

"Have you tried candied almonds?" I asked.

"Can't say I have. I know they smell delicious, though," he replied pensively. "They are impossible to miss at fairs."

I dragged him along as a new band went on stage, and Henry quickly finished his pretzel on the way, licking mustard off his fingers.

I dug out a few crumpled bills from my pocket and paid for a cone of almonds, which was from the only Christmas-inspired vendor around. Cheap decorations sparkled and flashed in green and red around the little booth, and it called for a selfie.

"Let's eternalize the moment my fiancé tried candied almonds for the first time," I said.

I smiled into the camera, whereas Henry inspected the candy. It was perfect. I snorted. My nose was getting red, I noticed as I studied the photo.

It was the night Henry fell in love. A slew of "how come I haven't tried these before?" and "oh my" and "this is fucking amazing" slipped through his lips while he crunched his way through half the cone.

"Can I have some?" I asked.

"I love you with all my heart, but I'd prefer if you got your own."

Great.

Before we decided to move closer to the stage, Henry had bought himself another cone of almonds to bring home—as if they'd make it that far—and he'd purchased a T-shirt with the "program" on the back. The whole thing was a charity concert, and he couldn't possibly go home without a keepsake.

On the way to the stage, we bought two more beers.

"I'm quite enjoying this," Henry commented.

I brushed my thumb across the corner of his mouth. Beer foam. "I'm enjoying *you*."

He kissed my nose.

The closer we got to the stage, the more people there were. It was impossible to get to the front, and we settled for a spot to the side about fifty feet away. That was when the nerves hit. *Mattie dropped out of college.* Here Henry and I were, enjoying the concert like it was an outing we'd planned to attend for the fun of it.

It was surreal to me. It'd been less than three weeks ago I learned Mattie was into music and playing the drums. It didn't feel like we were here to watch him actually perform. No, it didn't compute. I would've believed it if he were a roadie or something. Instead, he was supposedly taking the stage at any moment in front of a few thousand people.

"He's never shown interest in this before." I had to say it again. "Math, cars, engineering, the mechanics of things. He's obsessed with taking shit apart and putting it back together."

"Maybe that's what he's doing." Henry positioned me in front of him and tucked his hands into the pockets of my jacket. "Your brother is a bright young man, Zachary. I say we give him the benefit of the doubt and keep our fretting between you and me. For all we know, he's identified a problem, and he's dealing with it."

"By playing drums in a rock band," I deadpanned.

"I didn't say it was a rational choice."

I huffed and blew a breath between my hands, trying to warm them up. Henry offered me his gloves, but the end of his sentence was drowned out by the announcer introducing the next band. The stage went completely dark.

The crowd around us went absolutely in-fucking-sane, almost as if this band was one of the headliners. Were they?

"Wouldn't we have known that Lincoln and Adeline's son is a rock star?" I asked over the noise.

Henry spoke near my ear. "Her reaction was rather strange, to be honest. She seemed to be under the impression that Jesse is traveling with friends who are in a band."

All right. That was weird.

We'd have to address that later, though. A single light shone on the stage, and a man walked under it, carrying a guitar. It was fucking freezing, yet the man wore nothing but a long-sleeved tee under a regular one. Jeans, Chucks, beanie.

"How're you doing, Philly?" he asked as he adjusted the mic stand. Everyone went ballistic again, and the man chuckled. Two large screens lit up on each side of the stage, revealing a closer look at what was going on up there. The singer, Jesse, was older than Mattie. I estimated he was about my age.

He strummed on his guitar, a black electric one, and was joined by a woman who stopped behind another mic stand. A spotlight came on over her too.

"You know this girl." Jesse smirked, and the girl eased into a chillingly good solo on an electric violin. "And this fucker..." The bass player was next, a heavily inked guy wearing fucking shorts.

Jesse continued, "I don't know if you read this, but Liam just had a kid. So we picked up a drummer on the way, and I gotta say, he's fucking fantastic."

I watched a figure in the dark of the stage as he headed for the drums, and I realized I wasn't breathing. It was Mattie—it had to be.

"Let's see if he can keep up!" Jesse backed away from the mic, and two seconds later, they started the first song with a goddamn explosion. The entire stage lit up, Jesse's guitar riff as heavy as the powerful drums. The girl on the violin was fast as hell.

I'd call it rock with Irish influences, and it seemed technical— oh, that fucking word. No, that couldn't be why Mattie had joined, could it? He couldn't compare technical aspects of music to those of fixing a car.

As good as Jesse was, and he had a great voice, whiskey-like, it wasn't what I wanted the cameramen to focus on. I wanted my brother on the screens, dammit.

Nearing the end of the song, Jesse flipped the guitar onto his back and sang into the mic, the instrumental focus on the drums and violin. They chased each other, the beat revving up and going faster and faster. My eyes stung, reminding me I had to blink. And breathe. I should remember that, too. Holy fucking hell, there he was. Mattie and the drums filled the screens, and he pounded furiously until the last notes belonged to him.

"My God," I heard Henry say in wonder. "I have no words."

Neither did I.

Adrenaline coursed through me. The band didn't pause for more than two seconds, and the audience filled that slot with roars and shouts, before the next song began.

What the...? Something was fiery hot on my cheeks, and I sniffled and wiped my hand over it, only to realize I was shedding tears. *Jesus Christ.* Half stunned, half embarrassed, I quickly wiped my face.

The set continued while I battled against a range of mixed emotions. Mattie was so motherfucking talented, but it saddened me he hadn't wanted to say anything to us. Had I failed somewhere? Pride and confusion danced with worry and exhilaration, leaving me useless throughout their concert. I didn't applaud or get into the beat or...anything. Every now and then, I would feel my face splitting into a grin, and then I'd feel my eyes watering again.

CHAPTER 11

SOMETHING-SOMETHING DRUMMER BOY

*a*fter the show, I didn't know what to say, only that I had to get backstage and see my brother.

"Are you okay?" Henry asked. "He was amazing, wasn't he?"

I nodded. He was amazing, no doubt. Jury was still out on whether or not I was okay.

It took some elbowing to get to the front of the stage area, where a security guard was too happy to grunt out, "Authorized personnel only."

"There's a list, right?" I asked impatiently. I wanted to get past him before the next band came on and deafened me. "We should be on it."

He directed us to another guy working security, and he had the infamous list. Once we were through, we still had a busy area to search. Security, band members, assistants, and event personnel were milling about, going between the direct stage area and the two big tents set up against the fence. There were a few trailers too, and I had no clue where to find Mattie.

"Over there." Henry pointed toward a tent. Craft services was set up around a circular bar with a buffet and drinks for the crew.

I scanned the line and the picnic area next to it, finally spotting my brother at a table.

I stalked forward, watching as he laughed at something another guy said, and Mattie turned his ball cap backward. He had a white towel around his neck, and he looked like he'd just had a workout.

"Mattie!" I called.

His head snapped up, and his eyes went wide.

Two guys rose from where he was sitting.

"They should be here," one of them said as we got closer. It was Jesse. "I put them on the list."

Mattie glared up at him. "Oh yeah? When were you gonna tell your own folks about touring?"

Jesse smirked. "One issue at a time, kid. Today was your turn." He turned his head and nodded at me. "I'll leave you guys alone."

I couldn't find my words at first. The tent was heated, and I unzipped my jacket before I passed out. *His drink*. That was a good start. I rounded the table to join Mattie at his side, and I picked up his cup and took a sip. Plain Coke. Good boy.

"What the fuck?" I finally ground out and sat down next to him.

He flinched and dropped the French fry he'd had between his fingers and wiped his hands on his jeans. "What're you guys doing here?"

"Wrong question." My jaw tensed, and I had to make an effort to relax.

Henry, ever the diplomat, sat down on the other side of the Mattie and gave his shoulder a squeeze. "You were fantastic on stage, Mattie. Are you doing all right?"

"You left without a word," I blurted out. "What the hell, man? We had to hear from Ty that you dropped out of college and took off to tour with a rock band. Then you turn off your fucking phone? Do you *want* me to get an ulcer?"

"That's an exaggeration," he argued. "*They're* on tour. I'm just helping out for three shows until their drummer is back."

"Why didn't you tell us?" I implored.

He huffed a breath and pressed the heels of his palms against his eyes. "I...I panicked, okay? I was going to tell you when I came home." His hands fell to his lap, and he looked down. In that moment, he wore the weight of the world on his shoulders. "I had to get away, and if I'd called you guys, you would've stopped me."

"Stopped you how?" Henry's eyes flashed with concern.

"You would've insisted on resolving this with a roundtable discussion or something." Mattie grew frustrated. "I needed to get as far away from LA as possible, and the thought of sitting down and talking made me freak out." He blew out a breath and twisted his cap anxiously. "I told Ty not to say anything, dammit."

"I'm glad he did." Henry put his hand on Mattie's arm. "There shouldn't be any secrets in our family, Mattie. Zachary and I can't help if we don't know what's going on."

It was my turn to speak. "Did you really quit school?"

And there it was, the guilt and the worry. Nobody wanted to be a disappointment, and with the amount of pressure he put on himself, I could venture a guess and say he feared we'd be disappointed in him.

"Was it LA or school you needed to get as far away from as possible?" I guessed the latter.

He stared at his lap and fidgeted with his fingers. "I failed, all right? I thought I knew what I wanted to do, but my grades have been tanking all semester."

I thought I knew what I wanted to do...

Lifting my head, I peered at the stage area where a new band was making the crowd lose it.

I cupped the back of Mattie's neck. "You don't wanna do engineering anymore, and finding something else makes you think you've failed."

He grimaced and scratched the spot under his ear. "Maybe not failed, but I knew you'd be disappointed."

"That you took off without telling us? Uh, *yeah*. That you realized there's something else you wanna do with your life? You gotta give me more credit than that, Mattie."

He lifted his gaze and frowned. "Even if I wanted to try music?"

"*Anything*. You can major in whatever the fuck you want, little brother. Um, except Liberal Arts. No need to completely throw away the money." I flashed a little grin to lighten the mood, and I was relieved to feel some of the tension leaving him. "Look. You're not even nineteen yet. Whether you wanna take a year off and play gigs, maybe get a job or an internship, or you wanna pick up new classes next semester, that's on you. Henry and I are on your side, yeah?"

Mattie nodded jerkily and side-eyed me. His eyes were glistening, so I didn't push things further. "It would be nice if I could blame you two for this," he said and cleared his throat. "It wasn't until you talked to me at the house that I felt the walls closing in on me."

"It would be nice if I were in a hot tub right now, but we can't have everything," I said. "We saw you were about to hit a wall, so we talked to you. As evidence shows, it was about time. How long have you been pulling off both school and the music?"

He shrugged with one shoulder and took a gulp of his soda. "About a year. I'm so fucking exhausted."

"You learned all this in a year?" I was surprised. And I deduced he'd met Jesse at the fundraiser for Adeline's organization. "That's incredible." The thought hit me at another angle, and I whacked his arm. "A whole fucking year, and you didn't tell us?"

"I'm not doing anything complicated." He chose to ignore the latter approach. "There's math to it. A system. But it's possible Jesse told me I'm a natural."

He was proud of that and wary of showing it, I could tell.

I sighed and draped an arm around his shoulders. "The nipple ring makes so much more sense now."

"You read my mind," Henry said with a faint smirk. "Kidding aside, be proud of your accomplishments, Matthew."

"Whoa," Mattie and I exclaimed at the same time.

"We don't do that," I added quickly. "I've used his full name once in the past ten years. It made him cry."

"Yeah, that's only for when I fuck up really bad," Mattie said.

I pointed to him. "He had unprotected sex."

"You gotta bring it up again?" Mattie complained. "It was one time!"

"'Once it's all it takes before you'll discover the sounds a baby makes,'" I quoted Nan.

"For chrissakes, focus," Henry interrupted us. "Fair enough, no full name. Which is a shame, it's a beautiful name. Now, there was something about other shows?"

Good direction.

"We have DC tomorrow," he answered. "Then New York and Boston. I'll be home one day late, that's it. And you can talk to Jesse if you want. He's more anal than you two, and he's straight. He won't even let me drink beer."

Henry and I exchanged a look, and we were a little appeased by that. We all knew beer was the gateway to heroin and Satanism.

"You have to call us twice a day," Henry stated. "This is new territory for us, and we worry."

I nodded, debating on whether or not I should get another beer before we went back to the hotel. "Nothing wrong with three times a day either."

"Excellent point," Henry agreed.

"Fine." Mattie pretended to be annoyed, and he did a poor job of it. My guess was he was relieved and could finally unclench. "Is there something else? Should you insert a GPS chip under my skin?"

Henry seemed to ponder that.

"With the holiday season upon us," I said, "I'm disappointed I don't have any Drummer Boy jokes."

"Jesse has a shit-ton," Mattie groaned through a laugh. "What's the first thing a drummer says when moving to LA? 'Would you like fries with that, sir?'" Henry grinned, and I chuckled. "Oh, and he told me this one earlier," he went on. "Know why drummers have a lot of kids? They suck at the rhythm method."

I pointed at him and faced Henry. "We're buying him condoms for Christmas."

"That would be good, 'cause…" Mattie unzipped his hoodie to reveal the tee he wore underneath.

It said, "Save a drum, bang a drummer."

Actually, I think I saw a 7-Eleven down the street. Why wait till Christmas?

CHAPTER 12

JINX ME, MOTHERFUCKER, I DARE YOU

*T*here was a limit to the amount of travel I could do in a span of twenty-four hours without losing my fucking mind, so Henry and I stayed in Philly the following day. It turned out for the best, because we got to have breakfast with Mattie and Jesse before they were off to the capital, and it helped to get to know Jesse a little.

The next day after that, we were on the morning flight back to Seattle. Despite exhaustion and grumpy moods, we had stuff to do and didn't go straight home. Instead, we found ourselves bickering about the stupidest shit while we bought the last of the Christmas presents.

There was nothing like walking up and down the aisles of Target in a shitty mood.

"We don't need more chargers," I griped.

"I'd agree if you didn't misplace every charger you touched," he responded irritably.

I rolled my eyes and threw a couple gift cards for Xbox and PlayStation in the cart. My stocking stuffers were gonna be better than Henry's, that was for sure.

"Oh, honestly." He picked up one of the gift cards. "We don't own an Xbox. The boys use PlayStation."

My temper flared further. "Did it ever occur to you I was gonna get them an Xbox?"

He cocked a brow. "Were you?"

Well, no. But now I was getting them a motherfucking Xbox. I turned around and walked away.

"Mature, Zachary," he hollered.

"Bite me!" I called over my shoulder.

Knowing full well I was walking in the wrong direction —'cause the gaming consoles were obviously among the other tech stuff—I kept on going until I wasn't really sure where I was. I encountered women's clothes, so I backtracked from there. Shoes…kids' clothes and toys… I stopped, then took a few steps back once more.

I eyed a rack of pajama sets for young girls. The plaid flannel bottoms ranged from green-blue to gray-pink and were cute and comfy-looking, but it was the soft cotton tees that drew my attention. *Warrior Princess by Day, But Now It's Night-Night.* My mouth twisted into a smile as I read the prints. *I'm a Sleepy Future President.* I chuckled and touched the shirt. *My Plans to Take Over the World Continue Tomorrow.*

"Zach, what are you—" Henry stopped himself, and I heard him walk closer. Even my annoyance was too tired to go on, so I guess I gave up.

"I like these," I admitted.

He buried the hatchet too and pressed a kiss to my temple. "I love you."

"I love you too, I'm so fucking hungry it's not even funny, and I wanna have kids now."

Henry laughed softly and hugged me to him. "In that order?"

"A pizza might come before you right now." I lifted my gaze and kissed his chin. "I'm sorry I was a dick."

He touched my cheek. "I apologize for being an ass."

"Hey, those two go together."

Darkness had fallen by the time we made it home, and Henry idled in front of the garage, eyes trained on the living room upstairs. "Something is wrong."

"What?" Alarm shot through me, and I leaned forward to see what he was seeing. "What's wrong? I don't see anything." Then my anger got the best of me. "I'm asking for one fucking Christmas without shit blowing up in my face! Is that too much—"

"Hey—*hey*." Henry had laughter in his eyes. "I'm sorry, darling, I was making a joke. I was going to point out that we didn't have the red carpet out because the queen is visiting."

I blinked. And stared at him.

He pointed toward the window. "The luggage by the coffee table."

Okay. Coffee table—yeah, okay, I saw them. Four bags in matching blue with streaks of silver. I knew those. They belonged to Martin. The queen.

I dragged my gaze back to Henry. "You almost gave me a heart attack!"

That set him off, and he laughed as he parked the car outside the garage. We were gonna have to make two trips 'cause we had luggage as well as a dozen shopping bags. While we didn't have children yet, we'd made plans to drop off toys and clothes at Adeline's organization on the twenty-fourth, and I may have bought all kinds of pajamas.

"Isn't he early?" I asked, passing Martin's rental in Henry's spot.

Ty was due home tomorrow, and Martin was supposed to have arrived the day after.

Mattie was dutifully keeping up with our communication,

and he'd both called and sent a picture once they'd arrived in New York.

"You never know with him," Henry replied. "Maybe someone stole his car again."

I snickered and pushed the door open with my shoulder, and the sight inside the house made me raise my brows.

Martin wasn't alone. He was sipping drinks in the kitchen with my grandmother. Something was cooking on the stove, Christmas music was playing, and they were fucking giggling.

"What the fuck is going on in here?" I demanded.

Nan yelped in surprise, and Martin jumped. Then they were right back to giggling.

"Hi, sugar." Nan was having the time of her life, evidently. "Henry! There you are. Come in, come in. Dinner is almost ready. Martin and I are making lamb chops."

I dropped the bags in the entryway, torn between worry, amusement, and irritation.

"That's great, Nan, but you shouldn't be on your feet." Joining her behind the kitchen counter where they were preparing a salad, I took her glass from her and gently cupped her elbow. "Let me help you to the couch."

"Oh, don't be silly, Zach." She batted me away and stole back her drink. "You treat me like I'm over seventy."

She was over *eighty*. That was the whole point. She'd been sick most of the fall, and her memory was getting worse. It worried me to the point where my stomach twisted and revolted.

"Honey, do you trust me?" Martin asked, and there was understanding and compassion in his eyes. I swallowed and managed a nod. He and his sister had been through this with their parents. "Ruth and I are having a blast gossiping about you two and the boys. Let us. I know what I'm doing."

I looked over my shoulder to meet Henry's gaze. He nodded in encouragement. Then I eyed Nan's walker that stood by the fridge. Okay, Martin had it under control.

"All right…" I took a step back, only to inch forward again and kiss Nan's cheek. "I like your dress, Nan."

"*Thank* you." She smiled happily and smoothed down the red velvet. "Martin helped me pick it out in town today."

"He has good taste," I agreed.

"Except for in men," Henry said behind me.

His comment broke the tension, and I could excuse myself to unpack, shower, and get my shit together.

Our dining area was in a nook on the other side of the living room, past the fireplace, Christmas tree, and the stairs. And as I headed down, feeling tons better, Henry was guiding my grandmother from the kitchen, and they used the walker as a tray for food.

"This is the last of it," she told me.

I nodded, pausing on the last step so they could pass me. Up until now, I had completely ignored the dogs and Eagle, so I sat down on the steps as Diesel and Lady ventured over to see if I was still in a fit.

"You guys know I'm usually not a bitch," I whispered. "It's just been a wild few weeks, right? I want my family together and no craziness—yeah, I know, oxymoron."

Diesel huffed and sniffed my cheek before returning to his spot by the fireplace. Our little first lady wagged her tail as I picked her up, and then I think we both got the shock of a life-time when Eagle moseyed over.

"He's seeking out another human, Lady Mo." I reached out my hand, and Eagle stepped under it to get his head petted. "This is astonishing."

That was all I got, though. Eagle flicked his tail and went back to the couch.

Rising from the stairs, I carried Lady toward the dining area, only to pause again in the alcove. Technically, this was what I wanted. Ty and Mattie weren't here yet, but it was a start. Martin sat down next to Nan as he was telling her an inappropriate joke that had her in stitches, and Henry was lighting the two candles in the middle of the table.

Yeah, it was a good start.

"You still haven't told us why you arrived early, Martin." Henry began filling Nan's plate with roasted potatoes, braised vegetables, and Mary's little lamb. Setting Lady down on the floor, I joined Henry at his side and took my seat.

Martin poured wine for everyone. "It's wholly unfair to ask that question when Ruth and I have spent the better part of the evening sampling your collection of sherries, Henry. Where are your manners? You know my tongue is looser when I'm tipsy."

I snorted. "Your tongue is always loose."

"Yours could be looser, sugar," Nan pointed out. "I had to hear from Mattie and Ty that you've gotten engaged."

"Oh, shit," I cursed. "I'm sorry, Nan. I forgot."

"I'm sorry too, dear." Henry inclined his head. "We should have called."

"Let's discuss this in great detail," Martin suggested.

"No, no." Nan patted his hand. "Tell your friends about your promiscuous ways."

This was gonna be good. I grinned to myself and filled my plate, the food smelling amazing. Henry, on the other hand, was resigned and steeled himself to deal with whatever Martin said.

"Don't look at me like that, Henry." Martin lifted his chin, indignant. "I actually took your advice this time. You are looking at an out-and-proud polyamorous man, and I did everything by the book. Or whatever you said. I accept that monogamy is not for me. My love is simply meant to be shared freely and to many."

I pinched my lips together, barely refraining from making a slut joke.

Henry lifted a brow. "Go on."

"Well…" Martin waved a hand. "I was dating three fine men, and then it turned out your advice wasn't very good." I assumed his car-stealing ex was one of them. "They left me, so I decided I wanted a break from LA."

Henry took a breath and lowered his utensils. "Martin," he said slowly, "did you *tell* them you were dating others at the same time?"

Anger lit a spark in Martin's eyes. "But I was out and proud."

I laughed through a groan.

Henry pinched the bridge of his nose, seemingly struggling to keep his cool. "I cannot believe I have to tell you what being *out* entails." He released another breath and faced Martin. "You *have* to communicate with your lovers because, unlike your sexual orientation, whether you're monogamous or polyamorous isn't stamped on your damn forehead!"

"This shit is golden," I chuckled and raised my wineglass. While Henry and Martin were in the middle of the staring contest, Nan and I clinked our glasses together. "Merry almost Christmas."

Two days was long enough for me to shake the remnants of jet lag and travel stress, and Henry and I finally had everyone gathered at home. Nan spent most days with us, though she preferred to sleep at home in her apartment.

Up until Christmas Eve, all we did was lounge around the house, play games, listen to music, eat way too much, and turn the floor around the tree into a mountain of gifts. Henry and Nan rarely left the kitchen, unless Martin coaxed her to the couch with a bottle of sherry.

I'd never seen my grandmother so drunk before. Even Mattie was a little shell-shocked at the sight. And if she liked creative curses when she was sober, oh boy, it had nothing on when she was three sherries to the wind.

It was perfect.

We took family photos and Instagram selfies, we felt up each other's stockings, we took the dogs outside for long walks, we tried and failed miserably to make Eagle wear a Santa hat.

I got my snowball fight.

Today was Christmas Eve, though, and it was time to leave the house again. At least we weren't going far. Henry, Mattie, Ty, and I were meeting up with Adrian and Dominic to bring gifts to Adeline's organization.

Martin and Nan were gonna nap, chat, and knit, not necessarily in that order, so the rest of us loaded up the Jeep and drove out of Westslope and toward Ponderosa. Mountain cabins, lodges, and ranches morphed into mansions and trendy spectacles that sat on the hillside of the richest part of Camassia. It was where Mattie and Ty had gone to high school, and it was where the Benningtons came from.

"I was going through the photos from last night earlier," Henry mentioned as he drove up the mountain. "We should pick one of them to be our holiday card next year."

"Sure, as long as you don't write it." I looked up at the estate we drove past, happy I didn't live here. Sometimes, architects went nuts. "Then again, your handwriting is unreadable, so maybe it doesn't matter."

Mattie chuckled in the back.

"What's wrong with my handwriting?" Henry asked, insulted.

"It's all…" I gestured with my fingers, unable to find the word for the little swirls he made. Not swirls, but… "Fancy and tilted to the extreme. You write in italics, man."

"It's called cursive," he said with an eye-roll. "A lost art."

"Good riddance!" I grinned and wiped my hands. "Anyway. We can't have you jinxing us next year. You sent out, oh…two *hundred* holiday cards to your nearest and dearest this year?"

He knew an insane number of people. "You wrote how we were all doing and that we were going to spend December and the holidays together—take it easy and shit. Well, look what happened."

"Lord," he muttered, ignoring the boys' laughter. "Are you seriously blaming me for *your* photo shoot in Mexico? Or Mattie's spur-of-the-moment trip to the East Coast to become a rock star?"

I nodded. "You jinxed us."

"I wonder who's gonna sleep on the couch," Mattie said quietly to Ty.

"*That* would be Zachary," Henry informed us.

I puckered my lips at him.

"Damn it." He slowed down and checked the rearview. "You made me miss the exit."

I made *him* miss it? Pfft.

"We didn't miss it, did we?" Ty pointed straight ahead. "It's up there."

Henry sighed and put the car in reverse. "No, I was supposed to bring more coffee."

So we headed back to pick up some caffeinated dope for the adults who drank that stuff. And Mattie and Ty. They guzzled it as if it were Violet Haze.

There were only a few cars in the parking lot of the fancy grocery store in Ponderosa, and I halted Henry from unbuckling his belt.

"I'll go." I leaned over and gave him a loud smooch, then exited the car.

"I'm going too," Ty said. "I need floss."

Wasn't that why everyone braved the stores on Christmas Eve?

"I usually bring something extra," Henry hollered as I closed the door.

I nodded at him.

Ty and I entered the store and grabbed a cart for coffee and "something extra." Oh, and floss.

"I'll find you," he told me and turned for the hygiene aisle.

"I'll miss you while you're gone," I sang.

He laughed. "Nerd!"

Grinning to myself, I went straight for the coffee and picked out eight packs. How big was Adeline's staff? There were six full-time employees that I knew of. Maybe…okay, fifteen packs of coffee would have to do for now. Next, I moved on to cookies. The two times I'd briefly met Adeline's husband, and one of those times was at an upscale fundraiser, he'd been dipping cookies into his coffee. It was a grown-up thing. Henry did it sometimes too.

Twenty boxes of different cookies and sweets. Good ratio.

I cocked my head at the sound of Ty's voice in another aisle. His words were hushed and carried a note of impatience, and my first thought was that he was on the phone. Then, not so much.

"Because I'm finally happy," I heard him hiss.

That set me into motion, and I hurried to the end of the aisle and started looking down the ones he could be in—*there*. Great, tampons everywhere. And toothbrushes, toothpaste, fucking floss… Then Ty and his uppity grandmother.

"There's still time, Tyler," the bitch was urging. "You can come home—"

"Ty!" I jerked my chin and stalked closer. Relief and worry flashed in his eyes, but he had nothing to fear. I had this covered. Draping an arm around his shoulders, I eyed his grandmother. "Hello, ma'am. It's not every day I get to run into the First Hag of Camassia."

Her eyes grew comically large at my audacity, and Ty choked and looked away. His shoulders shook in what I hoped was laughter.

Mrs. Bennington recovered and glared at me. "How *dare* you?"

"Trade secret," I whispered behind my hand. "But we're done here, yeah? I'm sure you have a banquet to attend, and we queers gotta go do queer things."

"You are out of line," she spat. "Someone needs to teach you respec—"

"Don't utter that fucking word." I was towering over the woman in one step, sheer rage unfurling inside me. "You know absolutely fuck-all about respect. Do you realize how you made your youngest son feel for years? He was ashamed of who he was. Or how about the shit you put Ty through? What am I talking about—of course you don't know." I picked some invisible lint off her Jackie-O suit and enjoyed how she flinched. "Take your abusive, bigoted bullshit out of my sight before I really get started on respect."

Visibly shaken and angry, she took her basket and hurried away. It didn't escape my notice that her maid was waiting for her farther down the aisle, and she hadn't interfered.

"By the way, your nose job looks like shit!" I called.

I could cross "Harass the Elderly" off my list.

She had it coming.

"You okay?" I studied Ty.

He nodded once, swallowed, and let out a breathy laugh. "I can't believe you did that. Thank you, Zach."

"Anytime." I hugged him to me, knowing he was still struggling with some of the crap his grandparents instilled in him. "How about we don't mention this to Henry, though? He's all about turning the other cheek, and I don't think this qualifies."

He chuckled and nodded again. "Deal."

The only problem was if Henry had spotted his mother as she left the store, but when Ty and I had paid, bagged our purchases, and walked out, it was a casual expression on Henry's face we met.

Ty got in the back, and I stowed the bags on the floor of the passenger seat.

"Did it take that long to buy coffee?" Henry peered into one of the bags.

"Takes time to pick out perfection, baby," I responded.

"You bought Ho-Hos."

"Like I said, perfection."

He snorted and stole a kiss before restarting the car.

We arrived at the gated estate where Adeline ran her organization, and we had to sign in and show IDs to be allowed entrance. It didn't exactly ruin my mood, but it was a good reminder. The security was for the men, women, and children who lived here and had spouses or parents who couldn't respect restraining orders.

"You know the rules in here, boys." Henry pulled into the small parking lot and parked next to Adrian's car. "Some of these residents have severe PTSD."

"Yeah, no sudden movements or sounds," Ty answered.

I unbuckled my seat belt and stepped out into the light snowfall.

Upon seeing that Adrian and Dominic had brought their daughter, I grinned and held up a fist for her to bump. She was particular with touch, but we'd learned fist bumps worked great.

"How are you doing, sweetheart?" I asked, squatting down in front of her.

She smiled and signed something, and Dominic translated.

"She says she knows Santa's a lie," he chuckled. "Okay, now she's saying she's doing well."

"You are too cute," I told her and straightened again. "We ready to be fake Santas?"

With everyone carrying a couple bags—and Henry and Adrian putting Santa hats on Dominic, me, and the boys—we entered the facility. The lobby was a small space with a waiting room that opened up to the estate's common room. It was noisy and high-spirited, so maybe those who needed peace and quiet were in their rooms or in the TV room on the second floor.

"Hi, guys!" Adeline walked over with a camera in hand, and she looked like she'd been running around all morning. She was a gorgeous brunette and a fierce shortie, and she kinda needed to be fierce with the family she had. Not only was she wrangling a husband, two boys, a daughter, and this organization, but she'd been at it from a too-young age. According to Henry, she'd adopted Jesse and Abel when she was in her early twenties. Jesse had already been around ten at the time.

"How are you, dear?" Henry kissed her cheek and looked at her in concern. "If you need more help, you're supposed to call me, you know."

"Thank you for telling me I look like shit." She blew him a kiss and winked, amused by Henry's contrite expression. It was sorta funny. "It's all better now that Lincoln's here. He had a hellish deadline in Seattle—"

"Hellish client." The correction came from an approaching Lincoln, a tall dude with ink peeking out from the neckline and cuffs of his Henley. "Some people are cunts." He shrugged, then nodded hello to us. "Thanks for coming."

I grinned a little and scratched my head through the Santa hat.

"Of course," Adrian said. "Where do you want us?"

"Loaded question," Dominic joked.

I looked at him over my shoulder. "You speak my language."

"Okay, so we have two areas." Adeline had our attention again. "As you can see, everything's going well down here." Yeah, kids running around, parents talking and drinking coffee and having cookies. There were cartoons on the flat screen, a big tree, and music playing. "Then there's upstairs. We need two more people there, and this is going to sound so freaking bad, but I'd like to ask Zach and Dominic—preferably with your daughter, hon."

"Tell them why, wifey." Lincoln smirked and folded his arms over his chest.

"You suck," she whispered to him. Next, she sighed and faced us again, and she was visibly flustered. "We have a few newcomers—two siblings from Chicago, and a mother with three kids from Nashville. They've been through...let's just say, a lot. And—Adrian, you're one of the most caring and gentle souls I know, but..."

Adrian seemed to understand, and I saw him nodding. "I get it, honey. Appearances."

I finally caught on. Ink, beards... Lincoln, Adrian, and Henry were the tallest, all with stockier frames. If these people had triggers and bad experiences with men, they had to be careful when choosing volunteers. Made sense.

"You're immense, love." I patted Henry's stomach.

He narrowed his eyes at me.

"That's not what I meant, and you know it, Zach," Adeline accused. "You're a hell-raiser, aren't you? I've raised one or two, you know."

"Don't listen to the skinny man-child," Henry said mildly.

"*Hey.*" I stared at him. "I've worked hard on my abs. Both of them."

"I give up." Adeline threw up her hands, and Lincoln laughed.

"Are you sure you don't wanna ask us instead?" Mattie drawled.

Adeline was about to consider it, so I apologized and swore I'd be on my best behavior. I was here to be of use and help out. And Dominic promised to filter his language and not curse.

It was settled, and after another five minutes of instructions, Dominic and I headed upstairs with little Thea and four bags of gifts. We'd been told another guy was already up here, and if we had questions, we could ask him.

The TV room on the second floor was smaller and more intimate. The tree in the corner was minimally decorated, colors less sparkly and shiny. Three plush couches framed the low coffee table, and the sound on the TV was almost too low to hear.

There were no adult residents around, only a handful of children. The man we'd been told was already here sat on the couch with a toddler in his lap and another boy next to him.

"Coulda told me it was Casey up here," Dominic said quietly. Entering the room with Thea on his hip, he walked over to the man—Casey—and patted him on the shoulder. The bags were set on the floor. "Hey, man."

"Oh. Hey." He rose from the couch and smiled. "I didn't know you were coming today."

"Yeah. Adrian's downstairs." Dominic smirked faintly and touched the toddler's chubby cheek. "How you doin', Theo? You speakin' yet?"

Okay, so they were friends. One with a Thea, one with a Theo.

"He's calling everyone Dada, basically." Casey spotted me then. "Hi, I'm Casey."

"Zach. Nice to meet you." I headed over and shook his hand. "Your son?"

He nodded, and Theo played with his dad's fingers. By playing, I meant chewing. "My husband's downstairs with our girl. They were banned from coming up here. One is too solid, and the other doesn't know the meaning of indoor voices."

I chuckled quietly.

It was time for me to get to work. I excused myself and found a spot next to the tree where I sat down on the floor. All I had to do was put labels on the already wrapped gifts and write "Happy Holidays" on them. I had a kit with ribbons in case any curious children wanted to approach and help out. As per Adeline's instructions, Henry had wrapped them at home with a color-coding system to make it easier to see if it was meant for a boy, girl, or nonspecific.

I got comfortable and crossed my legs at the ankles, scribbling a quick greeting on a box with red and gold paper. The next was dark blue and had a bunch of snowmen on it, and they went under the tree along with the ones that were already there.

A young girl, around four or five, scooted closer with the toy truck she played with. I paid her no mind and kind of adopted the mentality I would if dealing with a skittish animal. She was shy and didn't make eye contact, though I could see she was curious about the presents.

"Hope," a boy whispered. He left the couch and stopped a few feet away. Was he her big brother? "Get back here."

The girl shook her head stubbornly, causing her dark locks to bounce.

I stifled my grin and added another gift to the pile.

By now, Dominic was doing the same thing I was doing, though he stayed on one of the couches, and he had Thea climbing on his back.

After a few minutes of silence, the girl spoke in a timid voice. "It's my birthday on Christmas. Adeline said I could pick two gifts." She held up two fingers.

"That's cool." I smiled softly. "How old will you be?"

She switched it to five fingers.

"Wow. Have you started kindergarten yet?"

She shook her head. "Mommy helped me count at the dinner table before she was gone. I can count to fifty."

Jesus, Adeline could've fucking warned me I'd be gut-punched.

"That's amazing," I told her.

She smiled quickly before taking her toy truck back to her brother. Or, who I assumed was her brother. He definitely looked protective of her, and he couldn't be more than a year or two older.

Well, I wasn't here to be impartial and a good guy. Sue me for playing favorites and being a sucker. I had wrapped some of the gifts myself and knew where I could find a certain pajama set for a future president. Along with the holiday greeting, I added Hope's name.

"I'm not equipped to handle that shit."

"Me either." I rubbed my hands together to warm them up and looked at the building in front of us.

An hour was what Dominic and I had managed before we'd left the second floor. In between shy glances and random comments from some of the children, we'd learned plenty about who'd lost their parents, who had been locked in a closet, and who had run away with Mommy because Daddy got mad lots. Now we were waiting in the parking lot, and Dominic was bringing out a cigarette from a battered pack.

"Don't tell Adrian," he muttered.

I chuckled. "Like he won't notice."

That made him hesitate with the lighter, but in the end, he lit it up. "I've had this pack for six months. He'll live."

Thea had bounced over to Adrian when we'd come downstairs, and it probably wouldn't be long before they all left. Adeline's staff was preparing dinner for the residents. And one by one, our families trickled out. Lincoln and Casey first, the former lighting up a smoke, too.

"I'm shit with names, but you're Zach, right?" Lincoln asked me.

I nodded.

"Can I have a word with you?"

Oh God, he knew I'd left an extra gift for Hope. "Sure."

He took me aside, and the twenty or so feet that separated me from the others felt like a fucking ocean.

He took a drag from his cigarette and eyed me, brow furrowed. "If I told you my eldest son was a social worker in LA, what would you say? I think you've heard of him—Jesse."

Thank fuck, he didn't know about Hope. Not that this topic was better.

"I'd say your social worker son is an excellent guitar player," I answered honestly. For some reason, Jesse—like Mattie—neglected to tell his closest family about his music, with the difference that Jesse was approximately ten years older than my little brother. I had no idea why it was a secret, especially with Lincoln being former guitar player in a huge rock band too. I mean, this guy was next-level famous, much like Sophie Pierce.

"That's what I feared." Lincoln nodded with a dip of his chin and stubbed out his smoke. "Thanks for letting me know." He turned to head back inside, and I could only hope he worked things out with his son.

Mattie was lucky he wasn't standing next to me right now. I would've smacked him upside the head in sympathy for Lincoln and Adeline.

Shortly after, everyone was done inside, and Henry and Adeline were the last to join us in the parking lot. Casey introduced us to Ellis too.

"I just wanted to thank you again for coming," Adeline said with a smile. "Oh, and one thing. By a show of hands, who snuck extra gifts to the kids?"

I widened my eyes.

"Shit. Maybe?" Dominic winced.

Relief smashed into me when I noticed most of the others had played favorites too.

"In my defense, I met a future president." I folded my arms over my chest.

"One kid taught me how to say 'Where's the library?' in Spanish," Ty said. "He deserved a thank-you gift if you ask me."

Mattie frowned at him. "Remind me to not get lost in Tijuana with you."

"No one's going to Tijuana," Henry said firmly. He read my mind.

Adeline pressed forward and made us write the names of the kids we'd given special treatment to, and she aced the motherly guilt. I felt properly chastened as I jotted down Hope's name. Or half properly, because I still took the time to scan the list and find satisfaction in seeing Hope's brother's name. Dominic had exchanged a few words with him, I remembered.

"Thanks, guys." Adeline checked the list briefly, then pocketed it.

"What will happen to the children?" Casey asked. "Hard labor is illegal, you know. It's not their fault we gave them extra stuff."

Adeline stared at him. "What's wrong with you?"

I kinda dug Casey.

Adeline waved him off. "Not my first rodeo. Everyone has a favorite. I'll just even the scores when William and Kelly come for breakfast tomorrow."

"William is the new counselor?" Henry guessed.

She nodded, pleased. "Adrian recommended him. He works at Thea's school, and thanks to you, I could hire him part-time. He's amazing with the children with PTSD."

"I'm glad. I look forward to meeting him." Henry put on his gloves, and it was time to wrap things up. It was cold as fuck, and the snow was coming down harder.

Before we parted ways, we wished everyone a merry Christmas and made plans to meet up after the holidays.

EPILOGUE

HAPPY HOLIDAYS, HO, HO, HO

"Two snuggles in two days? I'm speechless." I took a sip of my hot chocolate as Eagle planted himself firmly on my lap. "Back to dieting as soon as the holidays are over."

He yawned hugely before licking his paw.

"Yeah, you prefer the nights, don't you?" I murmured. No people around, no noise. The house was quiet and dark, the tree being the only exception. When Mattie and Ty were home, the dogs slept outside their doors, to boot. Leaving Eagle even more privacy.

He jumped off the couch—and me—eventually, and I reached for the box of Ho-Hos I'd hidden in the car earlier. I bit into one and thought about checking my social media, but I couldn't be assed. Everything was great as it was.

I scooted down a bit and leaned back, finished with my snack and hot chocolate. A yawn slipped out, and I gazed at the tree Henry had decorated. His eye for detail made me smile.

At the low thud of feet descending the stairs, I craned my neck and looked over the back of the couch to see him. His sweat pants rode low on his hips, and he wasn't wearing a tee.

"Hey, gorgeous." I smiled.

His sleepy expression warmed up, and he dropped a kiss on my forehead before rounding the couch. "I was only joking about you taking the couch tonight, you know."

I chuckled silently. "Someone has to guard the presents."

"Ah, of course." He sat down next to me and pulled me close to rest against his side. "What's the real reason you can't sleep?"

"I don't know." It was true. My mind was at ease, and I was happier than ever. "Maybe we went to bed too early." We'd kinda crashed around ten, and I'd slept well enough. For an hour.

He hummed, drawing lazy circles on my chest with his fingers. I kept my gaze on the tree and just soaked up the moment. Every now and then, I'd catch a glint in the corner of my eye from his left hand on his leg. It was his ring.

It made me flex my fingers and look down at my own ring. A surge of possessiveness and love flooded me, and I had to swallow against the overwhelming sensations.

"When do you wanna get married?" I asked.

"The sooner, the better." He pressed his lips to the top of my head, lingering. "Two reasons, one highly unromantic."

"Oh?" I looked up at him.

The corners of his mouth twisted up, and the crease in his forehead deepened. "Easier for us to enter the foster care system if we're married." He jostled me slightly in order to dip down and kiss the smile off my face. "I think you left a piece of you at Adeline's place."

Maybe. It was too incomprehensible to understand and process. I'd only exchanged a few sentences with that little girl, yet all I could think about was this need to keep her and her brother safe.

I was ready to expand our family, and though I didn't yet dare assume that Henry and I were the ones who would have the honor of becoming Hope and her brother's parents, whatever reason had kept me from sleeping earlier evaporated. Perhaps I'd needed to hear his reassurance that we were on the same page. That we were going to try to pursue this together.

"Are you terribly sad they're not twin girls?" The light in his eyes made me chuckle. 'Cause he was the type of man who laughed at his own jokes, and I loved the dork for it.

"No, it's probably for the best," I mused, humoring him. "We know what roles twin girls get in horror movies."

His body trembled with the laugh. "Indeed."

With a sigh of contentment, I faced the tree again and yawned.

"You'll make an amazing father, Zachary."

"So will you." I tilted my head and kissed the inside of his wrist. As he slid his hand farther down to stroke my chest, I blinked sleepily and caught a glance at the clock above the fireplace. "Hey, it's past midnight." I peered up at him again. "Merry Christmas."

He smiled and touched my cheek. "Merry Christmas, my darling."

It wasn't enough. I couldn't reach him the way I wanted from this angle, so I scrambled up and hiked a leg over his lap. He seemed to approve and pulled me closer.

"Much better," he murmured.

Combing back his hair with my fingers, I cupped the back of his neck and kissed him slowly. "I wonder how Martin would react if we put the other Viagra pill in his coffee. Did you flush it already?"

Henry groaned and nipped at my bottom lip. "We were having such a lovely moment, Zachary."

I chuckled into the kiss. "Okay, forget what I said." Then I deepened the kiss and coaxed his tongue out with sensual strokes. It sure as shit distracted me. Especially when his hands snuck up my back and he hugged me to him.

He went in for another passionate kiss, only to break away and breathe heavily. "I didn't flush it. We'll try it tomorrow morning. Imagine his face..."

"Oh my God, I love you." I crashed my mouth to his.

MORE FROM CARA DEE

In Camassia Cove, everyone has a story to share

Lincoln & Adeline — Path of Destruction
Dominic & Adrian — Home
William & Kelly — When Forever Ended
Casey & Ellis — Uncomplicated Choices
Abel & Madigan — Power Play
Jesse
Mattie
Ty

Cara freely admits she's addicted to revisiting the men and women who yammer in her head. If you enjoyed *Out For the Holidays*, you might like the following.

Noah
Power Play
Breaking Free
Northbound

Check out Cara's entire collection at www.caradeewrites.com, and don't forget to sign up for her newsletter so you don't miss any new releases, updates on book signings, giveaways, and much more.

ABOUT CARA

I'm often awkwardly silent or, if the topic interests me, a chronic (awkward) rambler. In other words, I can discuss writing forever and ever. Fiction, in particular. The love story—while a huge draw and constantly present—is secondary for me, because there's so much more to writing romance fiction than just making two (or more) people fall in love and have hot sex.

There's a world to build, characters to develop, interests to create, and a topic or two to research thoroughly. Every book is a challenge for me, an opportunity to learn something new, and a puzzle to piece together. I want my characters to come to life, and the only way I know to do that is to give them substance— passions, history, goals, quirks, and strong opinions—and to let them evolve.

Additionally, I want my men and women to be relatable. That means allowing room for everyday problems and, for lack of a better word, flaws. My characters will never be perfect.

Wait…this was supposed to be about me, not my writing.

I'm a writey person who loves to write. Always wanderlusting, twitterpating, kinking, and geeking. There's time for hockey and cupcakes, too. But mostly, I just love to write.

~Cara.

CPSIA information can be obtained
at www.ICGtesting.com
Printed in the USA
FSOW04n0710111217
42278FS